PROJECT CALIBAN

JASON RUBIS

SEVERED PRESS
HOBART TASMANIA

PROJECT CALIBAN

WWW.SEVEREDPRESS.COM

ISBN: 978-1-922323-76-7

"That a monster should be such a natural!"
--*The Tempest*, III, ii

PROLOGUE

Llewellyn County, PA
Fall, 2019

That noise again.

Eric Yates looked up from his iPhone, glancing nervously around the trees. The sound seemed to come from everywhere and nowhere, all at the same time. One minute it screeched out from the carpet of dead leaves his boots were crunching through; a second later it seemed to echo through the treetops, as though whatever it *was* was up there leaping from branch to branch, stalking them from above. Eric was frantically Googling wildlife of western Pennsylvania on his phone, trying to find out what kind of animal might possibly make a sound like that: like a long, drawn-out shriek, but not *just* a shriek. It wasn't just high-pitched; it had a strange booming quality as well, an eerie resonance unlike anything Eric had ever heard. If he were back home at his desk, or in bed with his iPhone, he probably could have found something to put his mind to rest. Some species of wildcat, maybe. Or a bird.

But he wasn't at home in New York. He was here in the woods in western Pennsyltucky (as his dad called it), tramping through the woods and struggling to hold his rifle so his father wouldn't see him pecking laboriously at his phone. The yearly deer hunt was Tony Yates' Big Thing, and any sign that Eric wasn't ready to turn cartwheels over the prospect of killing a buck of his very own would be good for a long, steaming silence, far worse than any yelling fit.

"Whales," his dad said suddenly. Tony was up ahead a ways, rifle in hand, scanning the trees.

Eric glanced up from the phone. "Huh?" He knew he sounded like a clueless idiot—another excellent way to trigger Tony's wrath—but he couldn't help it. *Whales*? He couldn't make his dad's comment parse with the world around him—the cold, the endless crunching through the skeletal forest, the bizarre howling, or Eric's own surreptitious research attempts.

Seriously: *whales*?

"Sounds like whales, don't it?" Tony said in his offhand way. "Like that thing we saw on TV, remember? *Whoo-ooo-ooo*. Remember?"

Tony didn't sound afraid or nervous, or anything but vaguely curious. At least he hadn't turned around and caught his nerd son playing with his phone. Thing was, though, the more Eric thought about it, the more he thought his father was right. The screeching *did* sound a bit like a whale's song. But that was impossible. The image of an airborne whale weaving its way through the dead branches overhead came to Eric and simultaneously made him want to smirk and shudder.

That was when they heard the gunshot. It came from the trees before them, too far ahead for them to see who had fired it.

"Whoa!" Tony shouted, sounding pleased. "*Somebody* got his buck!"

The whole question of what was making the screeching didn't really matter to him, Eric knew. Tony was still happily focused on finding a deer to shoot, followed by the ritual of showing it off to the locals. They'd stand around swapping flasks of bourbon and stories of past years' kills. The other men would be the sons of those Tony had grown up with, who had stayed behind in the little towns of Llewellyn County while he went off to a big job and big money up north. He was happier with them, Eric knew, than he ever was with his colleagues up in New York. Their wives baked nutroll for Christmas and made huge pots of *galupke* on Sundays, brought their husbands cold beers while they relaxed in the front of the game. That was how Tony thought life should be; it was a vision far removed from the players of Madison Avenue.

Another gunshot sounded then, a sharp *crack* that seemed even louder than the first. Then something that disturbed even Tony: a storm of voices, shouting profanity, followed by a volley of those weird shrieks and squeals. The screams were much louder now, and punctuated by a hoarser, angrier sound: a roar.

"The *hell*?" Tony grunted, and set off at a lolloping run, rifle clutched in his hands. Eric followed, as much out of fear of being left alone as out of concern for his father or anyone else.

After negotiating the maze for nearly ten minutes, they burst into a clearing and stopped short, both staring at the scene before them. A man in orange hunting gear lay on the leaf-strewn ground, his body twisted at an awkward angle. A rifle lay nearby his outflung arms. Another figure dressed like the first was nearby, staining the dead leaves red from a massive wound in his throat. A third figure crouched over the first fallen hunter—Eric took it at first for another man checking to see if he were still alive. A moment later, he realized the second figure was black rather than orange…but not 'black' as in black clothes.

It was covered all over in black hair, with patches of white around its throat. It looked up from the fallen man at Eric and Tony, and Eric gasped sharply. It was an animal, but not one like he'd ever seen before. It was two-legged, with a gigantic barrel chest and a heavy head set directly on the massive shoulders. The head was apelike, but it had a protruding bloodstained muzzle equipped with massive fangs. A string of what Eric gradually realized were human intestines dangled from its mouth; the thing chewed thoughtfully, then slurped the gut in like a strand of pasta.

Worst of all were the animal's eyes. They were round and protuberant, with no whites at all. Instead, they were a bright red, with mindlessly staring black pupils. The thing reminded Eric of some other animal he'd seen before, in a book or on a TV documentary, but he couldn't place it and didn't especially want to. At the moment, all he wanted to do was get away from it.

"Phew!" Tony said, waving a hand in front of his face. "Jesus, that stinks!" For a second, Eric wanted to break down into hysterical laughter. That was just like the old man; point a gun at him and he'd give you a lecture on how your pants needed pressing or you really should get a new pair of shoes. He had a point, though: the animal, whatever it was, had a scent coming off it like something from a raw sewage plant.

And they had other problems just now. The thing stood still, watching them. Then it fluttered its eyelids—for one lunatic moment Eric thought it was batting its eyes at them and opened its mouth, showing its reddened fangs to great advantage. It stood, revealing a height of at least eight feet.

And then it screamed, its head tilted forward. That weird, whale-like sound, but considerably louder and more aggressive. Tony, grim-faced, stepped in front of his son.

"Go," he said. "Back to the car. Call 911 and tell 'em we're out by…"

Before he could finish, the animal had moved on him, swift and silent. One second Tony Yates was standing giving his son terse orders and the next he was being lifted bodily off the ground by the animal, and flung around like a ragdoll. The last sight Eric had of his father was him lying crumpled on the ground, his limbs twisted at impossible angles as the animal went for him.

Eric ran. Flung the rifle aside and just tore off back through the trees. Tears stung his eyes and his chest ached. He made a little gasping sound deep in his throat, a *huuh, huuh, huuh*, he didn't think he could stop. He was ashamed of abandoning his father, and so afraid he thought he was going to wet his pants.

Just get to the car. Like Dad said. If you can just get inside, you'll be safe. They won't be able to work the doors and get in. He didn't have his license yet, but his dad had given him driving lessons. They'd always ended in red-faced yelling fits, but he knew enough to start the car and get back on the road. Then everything would be manageable, if a long, long way from fine.

Then something tall and black stepped out of the trees, blocking his way. It was another animal like the first, though his eyes couldn't detect any difference between the two. Without hesitation, Eric swerved to the left, but another of the creatures was striding toward him. Spinning around to go back the way he came met with the same result. He was surrounded—not just by the creatures, but by their weird, squealing cries.

Before the things got him down and tore him open, Eric glanced upward. There were more of them in the trees. They should have been way too heavy, but they were picking their way through the creaking branches with an impossible delicacy. He opened the camera app on his phone.

He tried to count them as they got closer and the stench of their bodies overwhelmed him. Two…three…five…he lifted his cell and snapped pic after pic. There were plenty of pics to take.

Oh Jesus, the woods are full of them.

ONE

The gal in charge of setting up readings for the bookstore had managed to find a huge balloon somewhere shaped like somebody's idea of Bigfoot. The thing—six feet tall if it were an inch—had been tethered to the base of the podium, and bobbed distractingly behind Marty's shoulder while he spoke.

Marty went with it as best he could, referring to the balloon occasionally as "my friend here," or "my esteemed colleague, Dr. Squatch." Luckily, the crowd—typical for small towns—was made up mostly of older women who'd been dragged in by their kids, along with a few locals with nothing better to do on a Saturday morning. Unlike the snotty hipsters you got in cities, this crowd was happy for an excuse to chuckle at the funny little man telling them Bigfoot didn't exist. The reading went off nicely, and praise God the Q&A was all but silent. No lunatics lying in wait to engage Marty in debates about "Nephilim" or lizard people secretly controlling Congress. Marty was looking forward to passing the afternoon getting quietly loaded in the lounge of the nearest chain restaurant. Then it was off to the airport and the next reading in God-knew-where.

Except, of course, nothing ever goes quite that easily. He spotted the kids in the line for the signing once it was halfway done. They must have come in late, because he was pretty sure the boy, at least, would have caused trouble during the signing. He was definitely the type. He was in his early twenties but he was sporting a full beard (when *had* those come back in style, anyway? Kid looked like he was wearing a chunk of roadkill tied to his kisser) and a faded T-shirt with the legend SOME OF MY BEST FRIENDS ARE CRYPTIDS emblazoned across the chest. He was clutching a handful of books and dancing around like he needed the john, peering impatiently over the shoulder of the guy in line before him. It was pretty obvious to Marty he was trying to make eye contact. *Wonderful.*

The girl with him had dark red hair in braids, and was dressed more for a hike in the woods than an afternoon at the mall. She was quietly pretty and looked as though she were prepared to wait centuries for the line to move. Poor thing. If she were the guy's girlfriend, she'd probably learned patience the hard way. Otherwise, Mr. Cryptid-Friend would probably be dead by now, knifed in his sleep.

Marty lavished time on each person in line, putting off the inevitable as long as he could. Finally, after a long discussion with a stammering high schooler (who had some pointed questions about how, like, could you really *know* Bigfoot wasn't out there? Cause the woods were so, like, *big* and all) Marty beamed up at the couple, turning on the charm and praying this wouldn't be too painful.

"Mr. Bloom," the boy said, a little more loudly than necessary. He slammed the books he'd been carrying onto the desk before Marty. The pile was a virtual syllabus of cryptozoology and Fortean texts, none of which, Marty noted, was *Bigfoot: Chasing the Legend*, the book he had come to promote.

"My name's Josh Carter," the boy said, speaking just a little too quickly (Marty suspected this was the beginning of a long speech he'd been practicing for some time). "I run a blog called Cryptid Hunter Blues?" He raised a hopeful eyebrow, wanting (no, *needing*) Marty to have heard of him. Marty kept both his smile and nod noncommittal, but that seemed to be enough for the kid, because he just went blathering on.

"I've taken issue with a number of your books in my postings. I don't know if you've seen my posts offering to debate you in public about some of your points in *Paranormal No More*?"

Marty fought back a grimace. He'd been through "debates" with true believers before. It was part of his job, though far from his favorite (*that* would be the substantial per diem that allowed him to drink off the top shelf most nights). It was tricky enough getting most people to accept simple statements of scientific fact. When they had a personal investment in the subject in question, it quickly became an exercise in banging your head against a wall.

"I think you're getting a little off-topic," the girl said suddenly. She was smiling at the guy, gently enough to shut him up without risking a tantrum. For a wonder, it actually worked; the kid looked down at his books, shuffling through them in an embarrassed manner. *They've probably been together a while,* Marty thought. *Long enough to know where each others' buttons are, and how to push them.*

"I'm Diane, by the way," she said, shaking Marty's hand. "Diane Rostov. Josh and I are actually exploring something very specific in the area, and we were hoping to get your take on it. Have you seen the recent news stories about *gugwe* coming out of Western Pennsylvania?"

Marty smiled. At least this was something substantial, something from the mainstream media, not some whackadoodle's hobby-horse. "Yes, of course. I could hardly help it. But if you want to get my take on it, we should probably start with terminology. The use of the word '*gugwe*' in referring to the sightings is, I feel, a little misapplied."

"Why? Scott Rolandson has been reporting creatures that match the Pennsylvania reports for years now."

"Well, if you really look at Scott's blog, Diane, you'll see that up to now, there's been very little there to tie his ramblings with actual sightings. It's one thing to talk about, say, smaller versions of Bigfoot-like creatures—those have come up all over the world, for decades now. But Rolandson offers no real evidence for his theories. He simply states point-blank that there's a kind of creature out there much like a traditional Sasquatch, but much bigger and more aggressive, with a noticeable muzzle. And he calls them *gugwe*, which is simply a word borrowed from the Micmac tribe of Maine for something like what we'd call an ogre. Sure, he talks about sightings, and even included that one ridiculous photo of what's supposed to be a *gugwe*, but where are the corroborating reports? Even in the little world of cryptozoology, there's nothing suggesting these creatures are even part of native folklore."

It felt strange to be taking "Rolandson" to task like this, since the fellow didn't actually exist. His blog—and quite a few others—was just a smokescreen, like Marty's books, designed and maintained by the same people who signed his paychecks.

"You mean until *now*, there hasn't been. There have been five or six reports now, all of them quite detailed, all of them describing exactly what Rolandson describes." Marty looked at the girl with respect. Diane's tone was polite, but aggressive and probing. She didn't display that wheedling please-agree-with-me tone so many true believers did. He sensed that if he could really score a point, she'd back down, more interested in objective truth than personal validation. She'd make a good reporter—hell, maybe she already was one, even if it was just for some small-town newspaper.

Still, he had his money to earn.

Marty snorted. "All the more reason to be suspicious of them. Don't you think it's a little odd that the creatures match Rolandson's *gugwe* so exactly?"

"Yeah, but what about those hunters who went missing?"

Marty paused. "That *is* troubling," he admitted. Four hunters, to be exact; two local boys and a father and son visiting from New York for deer-hunting season. It was something that hadn't gotten a lot of coverage outside Llewellyn County. "It's always troubling when real people come to harm. But that doesn't mean Bigfoot is to blame. I'm sure you've read all those books about people vanishing in state parks. Well, for each of those there's perfectly logical evidence pointing in other directions."

And when there hasn't been, we've put it there.

"I'm glad you brought that up," Josh said, pulling one of the paperbacks from his pile and brandishing it under Marty's nose like a cross before a vampire. Marty squinted at the book, and laughed out loud.

"*Monsters from the Mist.* Now there's a classic for you. Good old Dr. Bruckner."

"You know him?" Josh asked, sounding surprised.

"I wouldn't say I *know* him. Spoke to him a few times." *Nearly drove me crazy, too.* "Very interesting guy. Brilliant, in fact—just ask him. But his whole theory of people and cryptids disappearing into and popping out of 'wormholes' is a mix of lousy science and pure fantasy. I actually took his arguments apart in a book I have in progress..." Actually a ghostwriter had, but who was counting? Thank God these kids hadn't gotten wind of the crap Bruckner had been involved with down in Texas recently. That was the whole reason they were dismantling his work. Several world governments had a finger in *that* pie.

"Well, how about *this*?" Diane asked, taking out her smartphone and making a few passes over it, like a sorceress firing up her crystal ball. Marty watched her carefully. Her body language had suddenly become tight and ultra-focused. She had something big to show him, or thought she did.

A moment later, Marty was looking at an honest-to-God photo of a *gugwe*. It was blurry, but there wasn't much doubt that it showed an animal of some kind, not shadows and branches. The thing looked like it was trying to climb into the phone's camera. Its mouth was wide open, showing teeth like butcher knives. The eyes were weird—bright red instead of white or black, with contracted pupils.

"This was recovered from a cellphone found at the site," Diane said. "The phone belonged to Eric Yance, the youngest of the four missing men."

Marty kept his poker-face on, but inside his mind was racing. The site where the men had died had been professionally cleaned, but apparently not well enough. Some joker had missed a phone. He had never seen the photo until now, never heard that such a photo existed. Thing was, he *should* have heard. This photo should have been in one of the briefings he received each morning via encrypted email. That was the trouble with the 21st Century; so damned much information was communicated digitally, it was all but impossible to control. He had made that point several times to his employers, but that was like talking to his ass.

"Interesting," Marty said. He considered asking Diane to send him a copy of the photo, but there wasn't much point. If it wasn't already on every crypto site on the planet, it soon would be. He could just pull it himself.

"Yes, isn't it?" Diane wasn't *quite* smirking. Josh was watching with wide eyes, waiting to see what happened.

"Personally, I think someone is playing jokes with costumes," Marty said calmly. "That's my personal take on it, and I don't think it's in very good taste. Now, if you both will excuse me, I have a plane to catch."

"Can I give you our card?" Diane asked, already offering it to him. Marty took it, half-expecting it to read CRYPTO-HUNTERS INCORPORATED or something similar—complete with a yeti with big anime eyes, probably. Instead, it simply listed both their names, the URL for Josh's blog, and an email address in a sedate little front.

"We'd love to keep in touch."

"Absolutely," Marty said. He was itching to get out and give someone hell about the photo. "You already know where my site is, and my email. I'd welcome further communications." He wouldn't—he was hoping for these kids' own sake that he'd never see them again, but in situations like this making nice was the best way to make a quick getaway. It worked now, thank God. Both of them were beaming at Marty like he'd just given them each a silver dollar.

A few handshakes later, he'd made good his escape. He made his apologies to the bookstore owner and hustled out back, already on his own phone. A few minutes later, a limo pulled up outside the building and he was headed for the airport. While he waited for his boss to answer his call, he mixed himself a vodka and tonic from the limo's bar. It was barely past one in the afternoon, but he knew already it was going to be a long day.

***

"I thought he was kind of cute."

Josh shot Diane a peevish glance. "*Cute*?"

"Watch the road, babes. I didn't say I wanted to sleep with him, I just thought he was kind of cute. Chubby. Like a koala, kind of."

Josh snorted, glaring down at Daisy, who lay with her head in his lap. "Do you believe this? *Cute*, she says. Like a koala, she says. Guys like Bloom are the reason our civilization is being held back, and your mom thinks he looks like a sweet widdle koala-bear." Daisy gave him a languishing look and he took a hand from the wheel long enough to stroke her ears. The woman at the pound had said she was a beagle-terrier mix, but she must have had some spaniel in there somewhere as well, or maybe some basset; she was a total couch potato, never moving an inch if she didn't have to. Josh thought of her as his dog, but privately he knew she was just as happy to hang with anyone who'd rub her belly and give her snacks on demand.

"It's a little much to say he's holding back civilization," Diane said. She had one bare foot up on the dash, turning it idly to inspect her nails.

"Well, if not him, then what he represents. This whole 'skeptic' thing has gotten totally out of control, don't you agree? We'd have found whatever's swimming around Loch Ness and at least a couple representative Bigfoot species by now if it weren't for guys like Bloom. Our understanding of evolution would be ages ahead of where we are now."

Diane snorted. "For what? So we can put the lake monsters in a tank at Sea World and charge suburban couch potatoes to tour Bigfoot 'reservations?' Because you know that's what'd happen." She stared silently out the window for a time, watching the endless parade of fast food joints and big box stores zip past the car. "I'm glad guys like Bloom are out there. They provide a necessary challenge, something to push back on us." She smiled a little. "Moriarty to our Holmes."

"Your mom's crazy," Josh confided to Daisy. "Plus her feet smell."

"That wasn't what you said last…holy *crap*!"

Diane had pulled one of her sudden about-faces, pulling her legs in sitting bolt-upright in her seat, eyes focused on something far off the side of the road. She stabbed a finger at the windshield. The whole process took only a second or two. "What is *that*?"

Josh swerved to the right, pulling the ancient station wagon off the road. It wasn't just that he trusted Diane's instincts; when she thought she'd seen something, continuing driving was simply not an option. Once she thought she'd seen a Thunderbird while going out for soft serve and had simply kicked him until he pulled over. It turned out to be a jet, but that was beside the point.

"What? Where?"

"There!" Diane pointed again. On the left of the road, the burger places and car-washes had given way to a stand of trees and wide open green space. Staring, Josh just caught a glimpse of a dark shape disappearing into the trees.

"Did you see it? What the hell was that?"

Josh bit his lip. He knew what she *wanted* him to say, but he'd barely seen anything. "Uhm, a guy? Walking into the woods?"

"*Now* who's holding back western civilization? No *way* that thing was anything human. Come on!" A moment later, she was out of the car, darting across the road. Fortunately, this part of western PA was not exactly crowded; at least not this time of day.

Josh sighed. "Did I mention your mom was crazy?" he asked, picking up Daisy's lead. When they caught up to her, Diane was limping barefoot across the stretch of green.

"Did you bring my boots?" she asked, not once taking her eyes off the line of trees.

Josh winced. "Sorry. I was too busy trying to catch you before you got eaten by a Pennsylvania *gugwe*."

She flashed him a grin and reached down to pat a very excited Daisy. "Never mind. Us Jersey girls are tough, huh Daisy? Takes more than a thorn in the paw to throw *us* off track."

"So is that what you really think you saw? A *gugwe*?" Josh shaded his eyes as he inspected the treeline. The little forest seemed to be mostly evergreens, maybe farmed by some local for the Christmas tree season. It didn't look particularly forbidding, but he wasn't crazy about going in. Maybe what Diane had seen was the Christmas tree farmer. Maybe it was just some guy out shooting squirrel. Or maybe it was some nutcase who would take a dim view of being followed.

"It looked bigger than a man, I know that. Hard to say for certain, though. I only caught a glimpse. Did you bring the camera?"

"I..."

Diane rolled her eyes and started walking again. "Never mind. I have my phone. C'mon, girl."

Josh relinquished Daisy's leash and trailed behind them. As they moved into the trees, he kept his eyes down, scanning for anything that looked like a clue. Broken sticks. Tracks. *Spoor*. Anything. Not for the first time, Josh felt sadly inadequate as a cryptozoologist. He was a city boy and felt much more at home behind a computer than out in the field. Diane didn't have much more outdoor experience than he did, though she claimed having read the *Foxfire* books multiple times as a kid made up for it—as did, no doubt, her natural confidence, something Josh often envied.

Before long, they were deep in the forest; Josh was surprised by the silence around them. It seemed less and less likely that the evergreens were being cultivated commercially; the whole place had a weird feeling of being utterly removed from the world they had just left. Josh was about to remark on it when Diane froze in her tracks, lifting up a finger.

"Listen." A noise was echoing from deep within the trees. At first, Josh thought it must be a bird of some kind; it was high-pitched, but with a peculiar resonance that sounded distinctly non-avian.

"The hell is that?" Josh asked. He didn't like the sound; it creeped him out big-time. Daisy didn't like it either; she bunched herself against his legs, alternately whining and growling.

"Isn't it obvious?" Diane asked. Her eyes were bright with excitement and she held her phone extended at arm's length, ready to start taking pictures at any moment. "It's what we came here for."

Sasquatch? It was the obvious answer, but Josh had listened to hours of tapes scored off the internet of what purported to be "squatch calls" and while some were high-pitched, none of them sounded exactly like this. What's more, after years of blogging about strange unknown creatures, he found himself oddly reluctant to face the possibility he was now face-to-face with one. In fact, he would have given anything to simply taken Daisy in his arms and high-tail it back to the safety of the highway.

But he knew better than to suggest that to Diane. She was already padding off toward the noises, her phone extended like a weapon—or some kind of paranormal Geiger counter.

"It's in this direction. Come on."

Josh opened his mouth to suggest that a more reasoned approach might yield better results in the long run. That was when a twig snapped behind him and he nearly screamed.

TWO

Marty was well into his second vodka tonic when he finally reached Wilcox.

"Where the hell are you?" One thing you had to give Wilcox, he didn't waste words.

"Just reached the airport," Marty said, looking regretfully down at the melt at the bottom of his glass. There was no time for a third round, and that was for the best; he was going to need his wits about him. Still, a little more lubrication wouldn't have gone amiss right then. He wasn't looking forward to explaining the *gugwe* photo to Wilcox. By now, his boss had doubtless seen it.

"Good. There's a plane leaving for Pittsburgh in half an hour, and tickets waiting for you. Be on it. From there, you'll transfer to Madison, Wisconsin. Same airline. I'll have a car waiting for you there."

"You've seen the photo?" Marty asked. He was taking a chance, but there had to be a reason he was being summoned like this, and the photo was the most likely explanation.

"Just get your ass out here." The connection ended at that moment.

"Wilcox out." Marty sighed and pocketed his phone. He tipped the driver—not really necessary, but never a bad idea—and waved away the man's offer to help him with his bags. He made a point of traveling light and carrying his luggage—a suit bag and a ditty-bag containing his other necessaries—with him wherever he went. Wilcox's team could take care of checking him out of the fleabag where he'd been staying.

The first part of his journey wasn't noticeably pleasant. The Llewellyn County airport looked more like a garage, and the "plane" departing for Pittsburgh was a puddle-jumper whose pilot seemed to think he was competing for the Blue Angels. Things got marginally better from there, partially because Marty finally broke down and treated himself to that third vodka tonic on the flight to Madison.

In Wisconsin, he found a tall, silent guy in a rumpled black suit holding a white slab of cardboard with BLOUM scrawled on it in black sharpie. Close enough. Not long after, Marty was motoring through the Wisconsin countryside. It reminded him of what he'd seen of Pennsylvania—green and lush, though without the constant presence of mountains looming in the background. The limo's bar was well-stocked, but Marty opted for half a roll of breath mints instead. Supposedly, you couldn't smell vodka. Like hell you couldn't. And *Herr General* Wilcox didn't need to actually smell *anything* to be a bitch on wheels.

He had a pretty good idea where he was going, and when the limo turned off the main road and disappeared down what looked at first like a traffic tunnel, he knew he was right. The tunnel slanted downward, electric lights on the white-paneled walls lighting their way. Every now and then, Marty noticed men and women in white coveralls making their way along walkways set on either side of the road. Some wore hardhats and all had security badges hanging by lanyards around their necks. They paid no attention to the limo, preferring to scan clipboards in their hands or chat amongst themselves instead. Marty felt an impulse to tell the driver to hit the horn suddenly, just to see what would happen. He had a feeling it wouldn't go over well, though, so in the end he settled for crunching another breath mint.

While thus engaged, he also took a few minutes to download the *gugwe* picture on his phone. Sure enough, it was front and center on every cryptozoology blog out there, with breathless speculations on what exactly it was. Marty studied it for a moment and shuddered, then tucked his phone away in his jacket. Until his employer told him his opinions on the thing—which was the only reason he could imagine for him being summoned to the Cheese State—he *had* no opinions.

The limo finally stopped outside a kiosk where the driver presented a badge to a surly faced woman in overalls. The car rolled onward, stopping a few moments later in a wide, circular space, the entrances of other tunnels yawning on all sides. Signs on the walls warned of various dangers—none too specific, but all suitably ominous. Other signs advised that certain levels of clearance were required beyond that point.

The driver got out and opened the door for Marty, helping him with his bags. A moment later, he got back in and, without a word, drove down one of the tunnels.

"Gee, thanks," Marty called after him. "Yeah, I'll be fine. I'll just escort myself to General Wilcox. Thanks again."

He was the only human being in the area, so far as he could see. A few minutes of waiting didn't change that, so he began walking, picking one of the tunnels at random. He tried Wilcox's number on his cell, but got no answer. After another couple of tries, he stowed the phone and stepped up his pace.

This was not, by his judgment, a good situation. One of Wilcox's winged monkeys should have been here to meet him; that none had was most likely because they all suddenly had more important things to do. Which might signal some kind of trouble higher up.

And in a military-led organization that spent much of its yearly budget ensuring no one knew of its existence, that wasn't good.

The tunnel was lit with bare light bulbs set at regular intervals into the walls. The air smelled cool and clean; initially, there was a whiff of gasoline, but eventually even that faded. It was like being in the center of the earth. The dead silence soon got on Marty's nerves and eventually he began whistling tunelessly—partly to keep his spirits up and partly to signal to anyone who happened on him that he was just a clueless civvy who really didn't need to be shot, thanks ever so.

After a time, some unseen person began whistling along with him. At least, he thought that was the case. It was hard to tell over the shuffling of his shoes on the concrete. He stopped and listened, but all was silent again.

Experimentally, he lifted his head and whistled the opening of "Shave and a Haircut."

A moment later, the reply came: *Two bits*.

"Okay. Cute. Anytime you want to come out and say howdy-ho, you just go ahead on, okay, pilgrim?" He started walking again, both relieved and irritated.

"Anxious" came to join the party when a shadowy figure darted across the tunnel before him. Marty froze. He couldn't be sure of details, but whoever or whatever it was hadn't wanted to be seen—at least not clearly. The lighting in this stretch of tunnel was dim—he couldn't tell if the figure had come from another opening in the side or had simply been standing against the wall, picking the exact moment to make its presence known.

"Hello?" he called. No answer, predictably enough. "I'm armed," he said, which was a blatant lie, but what the hell? He started walking again, a little more quickly. A second later, he was aware of movement behind him and a hand fell on his shoulder. Marty turned and stared, his eyes widening. The hand had claws, and a distinctly greenish complexion. Its owner, viewed in the tunnel's uncertain light, was about his size, but walked with a noticeable stoop. It didn't look human. It looked like a B-movie producer's idea of a reptilian alien, with the huge, obsidian eyes of a classic "grey." It hissed at him, pawing at his shoulder.

Shock flooded Marty's system with adrenaline. He yelled and flung his carry-on bag at the thing, then took off running. He must have sprinted a good twenty feet before he was aware the sounds coming from behind him weren't hisses or roars.

It was laughter. Very human laughter, completely with snorts and wheezes.

Marty forced himself to stop running. He didn't want to—he would have been perfectly happy to spend the next hour running, until his heart burst in his chest. But monsters didn't laugh—not like *that*, at any rate. Turning, he saw the reptilian standing doubled up in the middle of the tunnel, supporting itself with a claw against the wall as it shook with mirth.

"Whooh," it said, laughing. "Whoo, Jesus! Your *face*, Marty!"

The voice was familiar, if a little muffled by what was now pretty obviously a mask. And it knew him, apparently. Marty narrowed his eyes as he made his way back to the giggling monster. "Jerry?" he asked. A moment later, he was punching the thing's rubbery arm as hard as he could. "Jerry! You rat bastard! I nearly pissed myself, here!"

The "alien" carefully peeled off its head, revealing a very human face topped by thinning yellow hair. "Ow! I'm sorry, Marty…oh God…that was too good! Too good! And I thought this was gonna be a dull day!"

Marty shook his head, smiling ruefully. Jerry Flynn was an actor who'd been pressed into service by Wilcox's outfit as part of their "misinformation" campaign. Guys like Jerry regularly patrolled caverns and certain lonely stretches of highway in their "state of the art" monster outfits, ensuring rumors of alien infestation and hauntings kept flying. Why the big boys wanted to convince the populace there were monsters while keeping hacks like himself in work producing books and articles proving the exact opposite was one of the many mysteries Marty had pondered over the years.

"What are you doing out here, anyway?" Marty demanded. "Last time I heard, you were scaring little old ladies up in Oregon."

"C.O.V.," Jerry said. "Change of Venue, you know...to C.Y.A. They don't tell me specifics and I don't ask. I just flap my arms and roar and ask politely for my paycheck. What about you? You out here to see his lordship?"

"So far as I know. Your sorry ass is the closest thing to the welcome wagon I got so far today. Looks like everyone's otherwise occupied."

Jerry nodded and began leading Marty up the tunnel, his mask tucked under his arm. "Come on, I know a shortcut to where you probably oughta be. You're right about everyone being busy today. Running around like their asses are on fire. Afraid their medals will melt, I guess."

"So what's going on?" Marty asked. He was glad he'd run into Flynn. The actor could be a little annoying—couldn't they all?—but he was as good a prospect for unvarnished intel as Marty could hope for.

"No idea," Jerry said, shaking his head. "All I know is it has something to do with the 'Original Mission' and you know as well as I do that could mean anything. The only reason I know that much is I was standing by a couple of the golden boys in the breakroom this morning, maybe taking a little too long to top off my coffee while they chatted."

"Original Mission," Marty muttered. "You're right, that *could* mean anything. How about this?" He took out his phone and pulled up the photo he'd saved that morning.

"Oh yeah." Jerry nodded, glancing only briefly at the picture. "They got *that* projected on every wall in every conference room in this place. Thing gives me the creeps."

"So it's not one of your crypto-cosplay buddies?"

Jerry shook his head. "Listen, Marty, I admit I was never much of an actor, but I worked with some of the best costume guys in the industry. Way better than these hacks Wilcox hires. I mean, those guys were *artists*, you know? And not one of them," he tapped the screen of Marty's phone with one rubbery claw, "not *one* could make something like that. You get to know the real thing when you see it."

"Yeah," Marty said. "It doesn't look much like the standard idea of a Bigfoot, does it?"

"Nope. Look at those freakin' eyes." Jerry shuddered. "Give me the heebie-jeebies. Hey, we're almost here. See that door? Right on through, just knock and press that beautiful kisser of yours up against the window. I'd let you in with my badge, but the security geeks would dirty their diddies."

"Thanks, Jerry," Marty said, offering his hand. "Nice seeing you again, man."

"Hey, look me up if Mr. Original Mission finishes with you early. You can buy me a beer at the commissary." With that, Jerry hobbled off down the tunnel, flailing his rubber claws and hissing dramatically.

Smiling and shaking his head, Marty stepped up to the door. It didn't look like much at first glance, but he would have bet it was at least three inches thick. The combination lock was like a mini-computer in itself. Behind the heavy glass window was a conference room filled with people. A small number were men and women in suits who looked as though they'd just woken up. Most had wheeled suitcases and carry-on bags, as though they, like Marty, had just arrived. The rest of the room were either in lab coats or sharp olive uniforms. Several of the latter wore maroon berets. None of the uniformed personnel looked particularly friendly, especially the slender, silver-haired man in khakis sitting front and center, shuffling through a sheaf of papers with an irritable look. When Marty tapped the glass, the man glanced up and rolled his eyes, as though Marty had come of his own volition, specifically to give him a hard time. He gestured at one of the berets to let him in.

"Hi Dad, I'm home," Marty said nonchalantly.

"Sit down, Bloom," General Wilcox said. "What kept you?"

"Stopped off for a steak dinner, sir. Gave 'em your credit card number, hope you don't mind." He winked at one of the berets, but got a frosty glare in response. *Things sure are different from when I was in the service*, he thought. Back then, the steak dinner remark always killed—at least with the enlisted men.

Wilcox ignored him from then on, launching into a rambling discussion Marty couldn't make head nor tails of. He slipped into the one available seat, between a stony-faced beret and a blinking, owlish man in a lab coat who looked as though he were frantically trying to figure out how he'd gotten there.

A screen behind Wilcox showed a map of the U.S., with a number of small red dots sprinkled over it like freckles. Initially, the dots seemed focused on the Midwest, but when Wilcox gestured and a new iteration of the map came up, they seemed to be moving eastward, specifically to the area around Pennsylvania. On the third such map, the Keystone state was all but blotted out by red dots.

"This is what we're looking at, people," he said. "This is our first priority."

This remark met with a low hum of apparent agreement and concern. The meaning of the maps was clear enough: something had been moving toward Pennsylvania over time. What that something *was* was another matter. Marty thought he could hazard a guess, but rather than ask for clarification he decided to wait a little; he wanted to hear it from Wilcox's own mouth.

The larger discussion continued, but though it made a lot less sense than the maps, it garnered a lot more nods and *hmmms*. Apparently, everyone in the room but Marty knew what Wilcox was talking about. Maybe he'd missed some preliminary explanation. He kept silent, doing his best to look alert and interested while saying nothing—the best policy in these situations, he'd always found.

"And this is our *second* priority," Wilcox said, gesturing again at whoever was manning the projector. "I say *second* only because she's somewhat less likely to rip your face off. But she's still dangerous and still a priority."

Marty leaned forward, expecting the next slide to be a blown-up version of the internet *gugwe* photo. It wasn't. Instead, it was a snapshot showing a youngish woman with short black hair in a poofy style that all but screamed early 80s. Marty guessed it might originally have been a Polaroid. The woman wore a white lab coat and stood outdoors holding something in her arms and smiling at the camera. Something in the smile suggested not just good humor and energy but a certain level of confidence, as though she was comfortable jumping into a photo at a moment's notice.

The something in her arms was another matter. At first, Marty took it for a young chimp—it had the long limbs and black hair, but the face was another matter. Specifically, the eyes. They were bright red with pinprick pupils that stared directly at you, boring into you.

Gugwe eyes.

THREE

"What're younse doing here?"

The guy was definitely a local. He was much taller and at least slightly older than either of them, with uncut hair brushing his broad shoulders and small, distrustful eyes. His boots and hunting jacket were worn and mud-spattered. You saw people in Jersey coffee shops wearing that kind of thing, but always brand new, fresh from the Surplus stores. This guy's clothes weren't just old; the cold wind carried a sour whiff of dirt and unwashed shirt off him. Josh could see the guy in a small, wood-paneled living-room, a deer head mounted on the wall, watching TV with a beer in his hand.

More worrying was the rifle he carried one-handed, the barrel pointed at the ground. This wasn't hunting season, so far as he knew—at least not for deer. The man didn't seem immediately threatening, but he still made Josh nervous.

Naturally, Diane stepped right up to the guy. "Hey there. Have you seen anything like, *weird* out here today?"

The guy gave her an unbelieving look, which traveled down to her now filthy bare feet—and put a squirming, smiling Daisy right in his field of vision. His face softened into a smile and he bent down, scratching her head.

"Hey. Hey girl. Yeah, you smell my Sugar on me, don'cha?" Josh hoped against hope "Sugar" was the guy's own dog, and not some local euphemism for something less mentionable.

"What kind of *weird* thing you mean?" he asked, straightening up. His voice was still cautious, but a smidgen less frigid. Daisy had a way of warming people up that way.

"Well, this'll sound crazy," Diane said, "but like a *Bigfoot* kind of thing. You've been seeing them out here recently, right?"

The man didn't reply immediately, but his silence spoke volumes. "One killed my dog," he said finally, as though that was all that needed to be said on the subject.

Diane's face lit up. "No shit? Oh God, Josh, did you hear that? He's Josh, by the way. I'm Diane. You've already met Daisy. We're cryptozoologists. Here, let me give you one of our cards..."

"Sam," the man said, sounding thoroughly bewildered. He took the card with careful fingers, as though it might suddenly grow jaws and bite him. "Crypto-what now? Like those guys on the Discovery Channel?"

He addressed the question to Josh, but Diane, predictably, was the one who answered. "*Like* them, but better. We actually have some idea what we're doing. We're not staged for TV. There's actually a lot of precedent for the idea that some of these things kill dogs and other domestic animals. Did you actually see it?"

"No," Sam said slowly. He proffered the card to Diane, clearly unsure of whether he was meant to keep it. "Didn't see nothing. Was last week, around eleven at night. My dog started howling to go out—I always keep 'em inside it gets cold out."

"Sugar?" Diane asked, gently pushing Sam's hand back. "The card's yours, by the way." She was taking all the information down in her head, Josh knew. She had a naturally good memory, and always insisted tape recorders put people off. In Sam's case, Diane thought that was probably a worthwhile assumption.

An odd, almost guilty look passed over Sam's face. "Sugar? Oh. No, Sugar's my other dog. This was Sarge. I mean, he was going crazy, scratching at the door. *I* thought he just needed to go pee. Should have known better, his hair...like on his back, it was all standing up. But I was tired and...guess I wasn't thinking too straight." He shook his head ruefully. Josh had an idea Sam might have had a few beers that night.

"Soon's I let him out I think, maybe he smells a bear. Sarge's a big dog, but he's old. Black bear'll kill a dog, it gets too close. So I get dressed and get my gun and go outside. I'm callin' '*Sarge*! *Sarge*!' Nothing. He went off into the woods—I'm right up there on Pike," he added, jerking his head northward as though that explained everything. "So I'm right there in the trees. I couldn't find him. Been looking ever since. Followed the trail down from my place down to here, but still haven't found nothing. But I heard *something...*"

"Like this?" Diane asked, eagerly pushing her phone into his face. She had the volume all the way up, and the wailing squeal that came out of it was louder than it needed to be. It clearly had an impact on Sam, who stepped back, tightening his grip on his rifle.

He's spooked, Josh thought. *Never thought I'd actually meet someone who actually had hackles, let alone someone who had them raised by something*. Daisy didn't like the sound either. She dug her front feet into the needles and barked fiercely at the phone.

"That's it," Sam mumbled. He looked embarrassed by his reaction. "Is that what they sound like? The Big…Bigfoot whatevers?"

"That's what we're trying to find out," Diane told him. "A lot of the recordings we have are high-pitched, but nothing that sounds like that. Will you do something for us? If you hear anything like that again, make a note of when and where and email us. You still have our card, right?"

The card had in fact been crumpled up in Sam's fingers. He coughed and smoothed it out, then nodded and shoved it into his pocket. Josh felt sorry for the guy, even though he was actually holding his own a lot better than most strangers did with Diane.

"We're staying in the Red Carpet Inn up on Percy Highway. Anyplace good to eat around there?"

Sam shrugged. He was looking antsy, eager to be on his way and leave these peculiar strangers. "Just the burger places and that. And there's Dolly's, over in Mertonsville. I don't know how good it is, but they sure's hell give you a lot."

"Okay. Hope to hear from you soon."

Nodding awkwardly, Sam paused to give Daisy one last pat, and then disappeared into the woods.

“Good,” Diane said, hands on hips. “So we’ve started making contact with the locals.” She sounded pleased, as though Sam had been a well-known university scientist. With that, she turned and started into the trees again.

“Where are you going?”

“Uhm, we’re still looking for evidence, I thought.”

“How about we go check into our hotel first? Wouldn’t the scent of the three of us standing together probably scare it off?”

“Good idea,” Diane said, looking down at her feet. “And I’d probably do better with my boots on. My toes are gonna freeze off. Come on, I’ll post the recordings. We can get a fresh start tomorrow.”

***

It took a good ten minutes of tramping back through the woods before Sam started to relax. He wasn’t much for strangers at the best of times, and the girl in particular had made him nervous. From the looks of the guy with her, he guessed she must have that effect on pretty much everyone she met.

When he’d first caught side of the kids crashing through the trees, he’d almost just walked away. He could have easily done that, without them even knowing he was there. The chief reason he’d approached them was to put a little scare in them—for their own good. The stuff about being crypto-monster-hunters or whatever they were had caught his interest, but if it weren’t for this recent problem with Sarge, he would have still sent them on their way—all the more quickly, in fact. They were both city kids, you could see that, and probably thought they were in that one movie—*Deliverance*, or whatever it was called. All Sam would've had to do was snarl at them a little. His gun would have sealed the deal—luckily, he and John Kolesar, the Mertonsville sheriff, had gone to school together. Johnny was alright. If the kids had gone crying to him about the big scary gun-toting redneck, nothing would have come of it.

But the thing with Sarge definitely made the situation different. Sam wanted to see if they knew anything about the screamers. Instead, they—or the girl—milked him for everything *he* knew, tying him up in knots until he'd all but run from them at the end. City *girls*, at least, were apparently not quite the creampuffs he'd thought.

He took out the card the girl had given him and frowned at it. Beyond their names, it contained little information he could use, just strings of letters he knew were website and email addresses. Sam didn't own a computer, though one of the guys at the shipping company had been after him to get one for some time. They had free porn on the computer, Sack-Eye had told him, that would turn your dick inside out. But Sam had little use for that, or social media, or anything else in that line. He was already paying through the nose for the damned dish outside his house so he could watch his wrestling shows.

He considered simply throwing the card away. Any other time, he would have done just that, but in the end he shoved it back in his pocket. Again, it was the screamers. Their sudden presence in the woods had turned crap upside down and Sam had a feeling it might be good to keep all the resources that came to him close to his vest.

By now, the trees were starting to thin out. He had been tempted to keep on with his exploration, but he knew it was pointless. Any screamers in the area would have withdrawn once they'd heard multiple human voices. Time for him to get back home. Sugar would need feeding, and so would Sarge.

Because Sarge wasn't dead—though not from any lack of effort on the screamers' part. That was one of many lies he'd told the kids, all made up on the fly. Sam's lip hooked up in a slight smile as he strode out of the last of the trees and headed up the narrow road to where he'd parked his beat-up pickup.

Nope, Sarge wasn't dead...and he was about as far from a dog as you could get.

***

He was home a few minutes later. Sugar started whooping it up inside the house the minute the truck pulled up the driveway, so Sam took a minute to open the back door and let her out. She ran around him in frantic circles, her stubby tail wagging up a storm. She jumped up on his legs and he patted her, smiling. He could tell she wanted her dinner, but feeding her would be pointless until he took care of Sarge and was in for the evening, so he picked up the bag of groceries from the pickup's front seat and headed out into the woods.

He'd grown up out here, in the house his parents had bought and kept standing up until their individual deaths—his mom of cancer, his dad disappeared in the woods. The grey paint on the house had started flaking years before, giving the entire building a weirdly organic look, like a growth that had bulged up out of the forest floor and was now slowly disintegrating. A few of the guinea fowl his father had raised still strutted around the yard. Sam kept them fed, but all but most had succumbed over the years to fox and hawks. The surrounding woods were quiet—sometimes ominously so, but Sam liked them. He had spent hours tramping through them as a boy, checking his traps or hunting squirrel. That had been before Sarge, of course. He didn't hunt as much now, and barely did any trapping at all. It didn't seem quite as much fun anymore.

He came upon Sarge where he'd left him, a vast bulk on the forest floor, mostly covered with an old tarpaulin Sam had dug out of the garage and covered with dead leaves. It wasn't much, but moving him any closer to the house was out of the question—Sam was in reasonably good shape but nowhere near that strong. And Sarge couldn't have stood being inside the house, even if Sam could have gotten him there—they had tried that experiment years before, shortly after their first meeting. Sarge had gotten inside the back porch and promptly freaked, either the smells of the house or the—to him—cramped space triggering near panic. At least the tarp would keep the rain off him and conserve body heat.

"How's the old man?" Sam asked him, stooping beside the tarp. Sarge didn't answer, or give any indication he understood the words, but his tiny black eyes turned to regard Sam silently.

"I know you don't like these," Sam said, digging through the grocery bag. He could already hear Sarge growling in distaste, deep in his throat. As near as Sam could figure, the fruit and meat he brought from the Shoprite still carried the taint of its processing; to Sarge, it apparently smelled *really* bad. But even this close to spring, pickings were lean in the forest, and Sam hadn't had time to give them the thorough washing that would make them less objectionable to his patient.

"You see any of 'em?" he asked, eyes roaming casually over the trees as he tore the skin off an orange. Sarge remained silent, watching his fingers move over the fruit. Sam was more nervous than he outwardly seemed; he didn't think the screamers would come after Sarge, even in his weakened state. He was much, much bigger than they were, and like Sarge, they didn't like getting too close to human habitation—another reason for Sam parking Sarge where he had.

Still, he had seen what they could do. Three of them had brought Sarge down, working together like wolves to bring down a moose on an Animal Planet show. Sam's gunshots had routed them, but they clearly hadn't liked it. The one in the lead—the biggest of the three—had bared its tusks at Sam, looking as though it were ready to charge. Finally, it ran off into the trees, but if they did come back, they might not be as afraid of his gun this time. He found himself remembering those weird red eyes.

He had no idea what the screamers were. He'd made several surreptitious research visits to the local library, but none of the few books they had on Bigfoot proved enlightening. The TV shows were even less help.

Once again, Sarge remained silent. He opened his mouth and took the orange, chewing it thoroughly before swallowing. He had developed a fondness for oranges, at least. Sam liked them too. He quickly peeled another two, then one for himself, and the two sat munching in companionable silence, Sugar settling down beside Sam's thigh.

He had been fourteen when he had come across Sarge in the forest. It had been deer hunting season and Sam had wounded a buck, tracking it until he turned a corner and came face to face with—there was no other word for it—Bigfoot.

Sarge was a good nine feet tall, covered in thick black hair. His face was bare and scarred here and there, tusks protruding from his lips. It was more like an ape's face than a man's—the tiny eyes in particular removed him from the realm of the human. But that hadn't bothered Sam much—he generally spent more time around animals than people, and he was well acquainted with how little a coon or a possum resembled their counterparts in cartoons or picture books.

Sam had seen the shows on TV, though up to now he had laughed at them, like everyone else he knew. And this was Pennsylvania, not Oregon or California, or wherever else they were supposed to live. But standing face to face with the thing was different from watching TV shows about it, or reading quick snatches from drugstore paperbacks. He was already wondering what he was going to say to the nerdy bastard from his high school class who had always insisted that they were real.

Man and 'Squatch had stared at each other, then Sarge had turned and run, crashing through the trees. But that had been only the beginning of a long and strange friendship.

After graduating high school, one of Sam's friends offered to take him down to Virginia, where he swore there was good money to be made in construction. By then, Sam felt weird about leaving the woods—and Sarge, as he was calling him by then. Not long after that his parents were gone and his course was set. Just him and the dish and Sugar and Sarge.

Sugar growled suddenly. She and Sarge had never gotten along particularly well, though over the years a peace had emerged between them. Sarge had seemed to understand she was important to Sam, and had never tried to hurt her—though Sugar made it clear she'd bite the hell out of Sarge first chance she got.

"What's wrong with you? Hey?" Sugar was seated close to Sam, her growls suddenly crystalizing into sharp barks. Small as she was, you could hear her in the next county when she really got going. Sam nudged her with his elbow, holding a dripping wedge of orange under her nose.

But Sugar wasn't interested in bribes. She got up stiff-backed, her nose pointed like a compass needle at the trees to the north. It was when Sarge joined her in staring and growling that Sam got really nervous. Thank Christ he'd brought his gun.

Several screamers came out of the woods. They were only slightly shorter than Sarge, though rather less bulky in build. Sam got up and motioned them off with his gun, but they didn't stop coming. As he'd feared, whatever had allowed him to scare them off last time wasn't working now. Their red eyes stared Sam down, daring him to make a move.

Sarge growled and Sugar well and truly freaking out, dancing around the screamers in wide circles. Sam yelled for her, but she kept darting in, nipping at the screamers' feet. That, Sam knew, could last only so long, and sure enough, one of the creatures bent down and snatched Sugar up like a bug. A moment later, it flung her away to bounce off a nearby tree and lay still on the dead leaves underneath. Sam cried out in anguish. Sarge howled and tried to get up, but Sam pushed him roughly down with one foot. The last thing he needed was for the old man to get between him and the screamers—he was just too weak right now. They'd hurt him bad.

Sam opened fire on the things. He hit one, but though it jerked violently, it didn't run. His other bullets flew wide of their mark—the screamers dodged them with surprising ease. All three were coming at him now, faster than he would have thought possible, hooting and wailing like something from a nightmare.

FOUR

The rest of the "meeting" was not particularly enlightening, at least as far as the identity of the mystery woman or her hairy charge. Though the berets remained in the room, the bulk of the discussion was by and for the scientists and media hounds present. They competed with each other pitching ideas to Wilcox for "damage control." Most of these, so far as Marty could see, were of limited use, since they depended on not just cranking out placating articles but placing them in local publications—a process that would take time. Still, the suggestions seemed to please Wilcox, and Marty could see why—however useless they really were, they represented actual actions that could be taken in real time. There was always something comforting in that.

Marty himself kept his mouth shut through the meeting, keeping his eyes on his notepad. He was writing down a list of the issues they faced:

Gugwe attacks in W. PA. Where G come from?

MW (mystery woman) – Missing? Absconded? Identity?

What is MW's role in W's operation? Connection to *Gugwe*?

He knew better than to try and ask Wilcox directly about the woman. The old bastard would keep his mouth shut and if Marty got too flippant, he'd probably find an excuse to stick him in a cell—he didn't doubt they had them down here.

After an hour of sitting and scribbling, Marty slipped out of the room, leaving his bags as a silent assurance to Wilcox that he'd be back. What he really wanted to do was try and find Jerry again, or one of his other old cronies who might be hanging around. He doubted they would have much information for him, but Jerry in particular was pretty good at picking up intel. Wilcox and his boys considered him a buffoon, and they were surprisingly willing to drop valuable information in the hearing of buffoons. Information Jerry would hoard like a squirrel hoarding acorns.

The problem was, once he was out in the hallway, he had no idea where to go. He wasn't familiar with this facility, and he didn't even know where to begin looking for information. Still, it wouldn't do to stand around looking confused. Instead, he picked a direction and started walking, doing his best to affect that self-important, vaguely constipated look he'd often seen in on men stalking the corridors of power.

It didn't take him long to find someone to latch onto: one of the guys in lab coats who seemed to be as plentiful here as the berets was striding down the hall ahead of him. The guy looked distracted and more than a little nervous, but after Marty had followed him down one corridor too many, he turned abruptly, giving him an unpleasant glare.

"Can I help you?" he asked frostily. "I think you might be in the wrong place."

"Marty Bloom," Marty said quickly, showing his ID badge. It would probably only get him so far, but he saw no reason to be coy at this point. "And you're probably right, but I'm one of the family. Media guy. One of Wilcox's 'skeptics.' Can you tell me what the hell's going on in this place?"

The man got a look on his face like he smelled something bad. "You'll have to ask General…"

"Yeah, the general and I aren't exactly BFFs. He's been kind of close-mouthed with me, honestly. But if I'm going to do my job, I need information, so I'm doing a little personal research. Let's start with those '*gugwe*' things. Where'd they come from?"

The man licked his lips, casting nervous eyes around the hallway. Against all odds, the guy looked like he was ready and willing to spill the beans. Probably things were going south pretty quickly here. Maybe he was on his way out. Either way, it was good news for Marty.

"Come with me," he said finally.

With that, he led Marty further down the hall. He passed his badge over a door and was granted entry with a loud beep. Marty followed, motioning at the unit with his badge but moving quickly in behind the scientist before it could engage. He saw no point in leaving a record of his whereabouts for Wilcox to bitch about later. He covered up the lack of a second beep with a carefully timed cough. If the lab coat noticed, he said nothing.

Behind the door was a lab—no different to Marty's eyes from any other. More lab coats were laboring away at workstations and laptops, steadfastly ignoring the two newcomers. There was nothing to indicate the nature of the work being done. The most unusual feature of the lab was a huge metallic door set in the far wall. It looked like something that might be used at Fort Knox.

"You'll need to change into these," the scientist said, indicating a row of white suits hanging on the wall. Once he got a suit down, Marty could see it looked more like a stripped-down version of an astronaut's outfit, with a boxy helmet of sorts for his head, and booties that slipped over his shoes. Some kind of germ protection, he guessed.

"How much protection does this thing actually provide?" Marty asked.

The man, secure in a suit of his own, only shrugged. "You're the one barged in here," he said wryly. "Little late to be worrying about any of that now, don'cha think?"

Marty's expression must have spoken volumes. The guy laughed.

"Relax," he said. "Seriously, you think I'd be in here if there was any danger of catching cooties? Couple decades back, sure, they were cooking up some nasty stuff in these facilities."

Marty's shoulders slumped. "Not so much now?" he asked.

"Not so much. Going the other way, actually."

"You mean...what? A *cure* for whatever they were working on previously? Why?"

The guy grinned and touched the side of his nose. It didn't do Marty a lot of good, but he could respect it. Hell, at that moment he found himself almost liking the guy.

He led Marty to the huge door and keyed a complex code into a small keypad on the wall. A moment later, he was sliding the huge door open. Marty goggled his eyes. The door had to be a good three feet thick, at least. The lab coat stepped inside, gesturing brusquely for Marty to follow.

Inside was a small refrigerated chamber, so cold Marty shivered. It was empty except for a hospital gurney with a body atop it.

Marty stared at it. It wasn't a *human* body.

Instead, it bore every resemblance to the creatures he had spent the past eight years patiently explaining did not and could not exist. It was a good eight feet tall, far more heavily built than any human, covered in a thick coat of shaggy, dark brown hair. The bullet-shaped head was ape-like—what Marty could see of it, anyway. Large pieces of skin and tissue had been removed from the face and various parts of the upper body, leaving a ghastly, skull-like grin. It had clearly been here a while. The exposed flesh looked desiccated and discolored, though that was probably at least in part because of the cold. Marty guessed the lab coats had been hacking away at it for some time, picking off pieces as they needed, as though the thing were a gigantic leftover Thanksgiving turkey.

"First time seeing one of these?" the scientist asked.

Marty nodded. He had a feeling the man was expecting him to be freaked out by the body, and he was keeping his eyes wide and face blank in order to accommodate him. In fact, he wasn't surprised by it at all. He knew the existence of these creatures was the whole point of Wilcox's operation. Still, looking at the body gave him a strange feeling. It *was* his first time, and there was something weirdly *illicit* about the experience, as though it were something he really shouldn't be doing.

"First time I saw it, I about puked my guts up," the lab coat confided. The man seemed more relaxed now. He stood stretching his arms and rotating his torso in a complicated motion Marty guessed was meant to loosen his muscles, but looked so odd he had to fight an urge to laugh.

"What are the cuts for?" Marty asked.

The guy smiled. "Sorry. That's above my paygrade. You really will have to ask General Tom about that, if you're that curious."

Marty nodded blandly. In fact, he knew very well what the cuts were for. Partially for studying the thing, partially for harvesting genetic material. Most likely it was part of the work they'd been doing here lo these many years, whether it involved engineering a disease or finding a cure for it.

"So what else you got on ice down here?" Marty asked, shoving the questions aside. "Chupacabras? Batsquatch? Living dinosaurs?" He paused a beat, then added with a raised eyebrow: "Any *gugwe*?"

The man laughed. "Oh, we *wish. Those* bastards are the whole reason we've been putting in so much overtime lately. And there are a crapload of them out there, too. More every month, seems like. I think they had that built into them back in the initial phases, that ability to breed lickety-split, like big ugly bunnies." Suddenly, his face hardened and he went abruptly silent.

"'Initial phases,'" Marty said, pretending the phrase was some exotic expression he'd never heard before. Then he let his own face harden. "Look, level with me. Are they local or engineered, like the bugs you guys made here?"

The lab coat scowled, saying nothing.

"Cause if they're engineered, it means you guys have been playing some nasty games above and beyond the germy stuff."

"Ask the general," he said stonily. Marty knew his luck had just run out. Nor could he blame the guy. Even if Marty had a badge, he could be planning on going to the outside media, and if it were found out someone inside had fed him information, it wouldn't do his career any good.

At that moment, a loud noise came from outside the chamber, a strident electronic roaring that climbed to a nearly unbearable volume before dropping and then beginning again. When Marty and the lab coat turned to the door, they saw bright red lights flashing in the lab and the various techs standing up, looking panicked.

"What's going on?" Marty demanded.

"Alarm," the whitecoat muttered, then, "Alarm! Jesus, it's a red!" There was real fear in his voice. He was out the door a moment later, frantically pulling off his germ suit.

Marty paused long enough for one last look at the skull-like remains of the 'Squatch's face, dyed red in the pulsing light. He thought about taking a quick photo with his phone, then abandoned the idea. Wilcox's men were sure to check his gear before he left—if he ever left—and being caught with such a photo wouldn't be a good idea.

Besides, he had other things to worry about now. He ran out the door without another word, hoping he would survive.

***

"Josh. Listen to this."

Josh looked up from his phone. Diane, cross-legged on the hotel room's bed, was hovering over her laptop with a hungry expression. "Listen," she said again, and pressed a key.

A noise came from the laptop's speakers, a wailing that rose gradually in volume to an unearthly pitch. It was like the noises they had heard in the woods, but less loud. Less *aggressive* sounding.

"What is it?" he asked, patting Daisy's head. The dog was relaxed beside him, caring nothing about the weighty matters claiming her masters' attention.

"I posted those recordings we took in the woods to CryptoCryptid," Diane said, making no attempt to reign in her smugness. "Someone just posted *that* in response."

"And it is…?" Josh asked, irritated.

"He says it's some kind of lemur," Diane said, lowering her head to peer at the screen. "An '*indri.*'"

"Lemurs?" Josh frowned. "Don't they all live on some island somewhere?"

"Madagascar. Off the southern coast of Africa. The guy who posted it lived there for a while, apparently. He said you'd go out in the morning and they'd all be in the trees singing like that. Like whales, almost."

"In the *trees*?" Josh asked. Something about the idea of creatures capable of such noises congregating in the treetops was oddly disturbing. "Well, if they're all in Madagascar, why did *we* hear them in western Pennsylvania? And what do lemurs have to do with Bigfoot? Aren't they all little cuddly critters with big eyes?"

"Well, *indri* are pretty big, apparently," Diane said. "And the cries we heard aren't actually identical with their 'singing.' This guy works at a primate research lab and he's offered to run some analysis on the recordings."

"Yeah, but still," Josh countered, shaking his head. "Those *indri* recordings are more like what we heard than anything else. What do *lemurs* have to do with Bigfoot-type cryptids that make people disappear?"

"Come on, Josh! You're a good Fortean, right? This is exactly the kind of mystery we thrive on!" Diane shut her laptop with a snap. "Now I say let's go check out this Dolly's place Sam told us about. I'm hungry."

Josh nodded, staring glumly down at his phone. He had just Googled "*indri*" and was looking at a number of photos of very odd-looking primates, long-limbed with doglike muzzles and big, staring red eyes.

He shuddered as he pocketed the phone and got up to get his jacket. God, but those eyes were *creepy*.

***

They found Dolly's without any trouble, shortly after passing a sign that informed them they had just crossed into Mertonsville. The restaurant sat on a corner of what Josh assumed was the town's main drag, a block that also housed the post office and a hardware store.

Inside, Dolly's wasn't exactly hopping. Only three of the tables were occupied, one by a couple of guys who looked they might be Sam's bigger, rougher brothers, another by a family who were silently working their way through a large pepperoni pie, and a third by a lone, thin woman with short, grey-shot black hair who sat reading a paper.

The place's décor looked like a half-hearted attempt to replicate the vibe of a '50s diner had been abandoned in favor of throwing up whatever bits of bric-a-brac the owners could find in their attic. The walls were covered with photos of various local high school classes from the early '60s onward.

A tired-looking girl presented them with menus. "What's good here?" Diane asked brightly.

The girl shrugged. She didn't seem unpleasant, just on the verge of falling over. *She probably works two or three other jobs just to survive*, Josh thought glumly.

"People like the burgers," the waitress said, pointing with her pen at Diane's open menu. In fact, the burger section represented the lion's share of the menu's offerings, in addition to pizza and a small section of "home-cookin'," which included meatloaf and fried chicken.

"We're out of chicken," the waitress warned. "And meatloaf."

Both Diane and Josh opted for burger platters and cokes, and sat looking around. The folks at the other tables gave them single incurious glances and went back to their food. The woman in back didn't look up at all.

"Think any of these guys have had any sightings?" Diane asked eagerly.

"Doubt it," Josh said. He was starting to feel like they were spinning their wheels. This was just another dried-up town in coal-mining country. The real cryptid action would be out in the woods. Back home, he had been champing at the bit to get out here and do some hands-on investigation but now the prospect of tramping around the woods didn't appeal to him at all. *Maybe I am just an armchair cryptozoologist*, he thought. *And is that so bad? These days, you can do a lot of research online, without even leaving your house.*

Suddenly, the bell over the restaurant's door tinkled—or clanked, might have been a better description. "Oh my God!" Diane gasped.

Josh looked up and saw Sam, their first contact, enter the restaurant, carrying something wrapped in what looked like bloody towels. The man's eyes were wide and panicked-looking, and there was blood on his cheek.

The other patrons stared at him. A heavyset guy in an apron came out of the kitchen. "Sam?" the man asked. "What in hell happened?"

Sam paid him no attention. "Dr. Smith!" he called. "Dr. Smith, it's Sugar!"

The woman at the rear table was already running to him. "Oh my God," she said. "Oh my God, what happened to her?"

Sam opened his mouth, then shut it quickly. Josh thought the man might have spotted them at the table just before he clammed up, but a moment later he wasn't so sure.

"Bear," he said quickly. "Bear got her. I went to your office and Carol said you were here."

The woman had reached his side and was stroking Sugar's head. The dog's tail beat feebly. Dr. Smith nodded. "Let's get back there. I can't do anything for her here."

"Can we help?" Diane asked suddenly. Josh stared at Diane, along with everyone else in the restaurant, it seemed.

Josh winced. "Diane, I don't think…"

"We're friends of Sam's," Diane said. "Right, Sam?"

Sam stared at her as though she had just stepped out of a flying saucer.

"Come on, or don't," Dr. Smith said, hustling Sam out the restaurant door. "But we gotta go." Glancing doubtfully back at Diane, she asked, "Do you even know where my office is?"

"It's Dr. Smith, right?" Diane asked eagerly, tugging on her jacket. "We can look it up on my GPS. Come on, Josh."

A moment later, she had followed Sam and the doctor out. Josh stood looking helplessly at the other patrons, then at the waitress, who had come out with a tray loaded down with fries and two mountainous burgers.

"Younse want these to go?" she asked helpfully.

FIVE

Outside the lab, the corridor was filled with thick, eye-stinging smoke. There were also a number of lab coats running frantically in one direction or another, some clutching handfuls of files to their chest or hobbling along under the weight of cardboard boxes.

Marty began walking quickly in what he remembered as the direction he'd come from—which was the same direction most of the lab coats had chosen. He wasn't particularly keen on running into Wilcox—which was pretty much a given if he went on—but he had to go somewhere, and this would at least get him back among human beings. Probably Wilcox wouldn't have time to even think about him, if he were lucky.

In the meantime, he tried to get a fix on the smoke. It was increasingly thick and black, and had an unmistakable tang of burning rubber. *Somebody's burning tires*, he thought dazedly, coughing. The fumes were billowing into the corridor from vents placed at even intervals along the ceiling. A terrorist attack? He couldn't think of anyone else who'd want to put a hurt on Wilcox's facility, but it didn't make much sense. Surely there'd be more effective ways of bringing the place to heel than piling up old tires by the air vents and setting them afire—anthrax, for example, or a nice little bomb.

As Marty got closer to the conference room, the corridor filled with red berets, some of whom were bearing nasty-looking firearms. They were approaching the lab coats and directing them into side corridors—though if they were just a bit rougher about it, you would have had to say kicking their asses down the corridors instead.

Marty went up to the meanest-looking of the lot, the young fellow who'd given him contemptuous looks in the conference room. "What's going on?" he demanded.

"Please go with the others, sir. That way." The man didn't actually shove Marty with his gun, but he looked as though he would have dearly liked to. He didn't look scared, Marty realized, but rather eager. Practically bouncing on the toes of his boots. *He wants to get the civilians out of the way so he can start playing soldier-boy*. But with who?

Someone behind him screamed suddenly—there was no telling if it were a man or a woman, but they were clearly scared witless. Marty saw four dark figures running toward

them out of the smoke. They weren't fully erect, rather running with hunched shoulders with an odd loping gait. He couldn't tell whether they were wearing dark uniforms of some kind or if they were—as he suspected—*gugwe*.

The beret was suddenly shouting into a communication device he'd taken from his belt. Much of it was coded babble, but Marty caught the word *breach* repeated several times. The beret shouldered him out of the way, hard enough to make him stumble, and coolly aimed his gun at the approaching figures. Several of the other berets took up positions on his right and left, their own arms held ready, but not raised as yet.

By now, Marty could see he had been right. The invaders *were gugwe*. Somehow he hadn't expected them to be so big, but they were; they were *huge*. The reason they had been slumped over, Marty saw, was because otherwise their bullet-shaped heads would have scraped the ceiling. They carried what he first took to be wooden clubs, *a la* cartoon cavemen. But they weren't clubs. He saw that when the big *gugwe* in front raised his and a viciously loud *crack* echoed in the corridor. The beret dropped his gun and fell back several steps, a startled expression on his face. He fell to the floor, feeling at his side. The poor guy looked like a kid caught out in a game of cops and robbers.

Holy crap, Marty thought. *They've got guns. They're* armed.

The other berets were firing by now, and one of the *gugwe* fell, tearing at its breast as though affronted by the pain. The others started firing and several berets dropped.

This initial triumph seemed to excite the *gugwe*; the one in front screamed, opening its wolfish jaws and revealing yellowed, curved tusks. The others joined it a moment later, all shaking their firearms in the air and howling.

And not just howling, but grunting deep in their throats, each grunt a single syllable.

"Hut. Hut-hut! *Hut*!"

Are you kidding me? It's not enough they've got guns, they're actually going "hut-hut" like a bunch of dogfaces taking a beach? Literal *dogfaces.*

Their guns, Marty saw, were of different makes and none of them looked in particularly good condition. They looked as though they'd been buried for a long time and just recently dug up. Then they advanced on the fallen soldier, still showing their teeth and fluttering their eyelids in a way that looked weirdly as though they were batting their eyes.

That was all the observation Marty had time for. He tore off down the corridor, which by now was empty. The electric lights overhead allowed him to easily find his way, but they also made him feel painfully visible. He expected at any moment to feel a bullet bury itself in his shoulder.

Please God, he thought desperately. *Just let me get out of this and I'll go into real estate, I* promise. His legs had already carried him to the point where the sounds of battle had faded, but a stitch was burning in his side, and he was breathing like a steam engine. There wasn't much smoke in the tunnel, but there was enough to make him nauseous; he knew that any moment he might have to stop and throw up the few drinks he had indulged in on the plane.

"Marty!" The voice burst from one of the side tunnels and Marty allowed himself to come to a stumbling, inelegant halt. He avoided throwing up—barely—but stood gripping his knees, sweating and gasping for breath.

Jerry ran out of the tunnel. The alien mask was gone, but he was still wearing the claws and the piece covering his upper body. Marty wanted to laugh, but he was afraid if he did he'd lose it for real. "Come on," Jerry said, tugging at Marty's arm. "Doo-doo's hit the fan, brah. We gotta *move*."

Marty let himself be maneuvered into the side-tunnel, where a vehicle something like a cross between a golf cart and a moon-buggy was waiting. Another couple of guys were inside, one behind the wheel. They didn't wear alien gear, but Marty didn't doubt they were Jerry's colleagues. They certainly didn't look like either military or scientists.

"That your buddy?" the guy behind the wheel asked. Jerry nodded as he helped Marty into one of the rear seats.

"Anybody else you wanna pick up? Your sister, or…?"

"Don't be an ass, Cliff. Just *drive*."

Cliff nodded tightly and moments later they were flying down the tunnel. Marty didn't ask if Cliff actually knew how to drive the cart—at best, he'd had maybe a lesson or two. Several times they nearly crashed into a wall. But they were moving, and that was all Marty cared about.

"Where'd those things come from?" Marty asked. "I thought Wisconsin was the land of cheese, not gun-wielding cryptids."

"You got me, dude," Jerry said, shaking his head. "They must've come out of the woods. You know, they're the reason this place was set up to begin with, back in the '70s. Try talking to

Wilcox about it, though. Still, I was starting to hear rumors recently—Chuck up there saw a couple lurking around the trees just the other day."

The guy sitting shotgun turned and gave them a bug-eyed, frightened stare. "There was like a whole dozen of 'em, man! I told some of Wilcox's guys, and they were all like, 'Huh. Well, we'll look into it.' Assholes."

The buggy hit a bump, causing Marty's rump to briefly part ways with the seat. He came back down with a grunt. "So where we going, anyway?"

"I don't know about anybody else," Cliff said. "But *I'm* headed for the parking lot. Once I'm in my own car, I couldn't give a shit what anybody else does."

"Amen, brother," Jerry said. "I'm going back to L.A. I don't care, man, I'll be one of those guys playing Captain Jack on the Boulevard. Or Spidey, or whoever. Beats getting shot in the ass by Bigfoot."

"What about Wilcox?" Marty asked. "Don't you guys have some kind of contract with him?"

"Gotta find me first, sir."

Marty nodded reflectively. He couldn't blame Jerry, but he had a feeling ditching Wilcox's operation wasn't going to be as easy as just walking away. He had no idea how deep this whole *gugwe* thing went, but it had to be deep. And Uncle Sam wasn't much for deserters.

Even so, he had no interest in going back.

The four lapsed into silence for a time. A few minutes later, Cliff brought the buggy out of a tunnel-mouth into a parking lot. A single narrow road connected it to a larger highway—Marty guessed any civilian driving by the place wouldn't look twice at it. The road was empty, but a few lab coats were hurriedly getting into their cars and pulling away.

Jerry exchanged hurried goodbyes with his colleagues and pulled a set of keys from inside his alien costume.

"I can drop you somewhere," he told Marty.

"Anywhere I can get a motel room or a cab," Marty told him. He was already thinking furiously, though it didn't seem to be getting him anywhere. Mostly, he was wondering if any of them could ever really get away from Wilcox.

***

Whatever had attacked Sugar had really done a number on her. The odd thing was, her injuries were mostly internal, almost as if whatever had got to her had been trying to crush her—or had just thrown her violently against a wall. Josh didn't know much about bears, but he'd never heard of one prone to such behavior.

After X-rays and much bandaging, Dr. Smith's assistant Carol—a quiet-spoken young woman with dark hair—carried her off to the kennels behind the office for some rest. Sam stood by the door of the operating room throughout the process, watching silently as his dog was treated. Josh could feel anger coming off him in cold waves. Josh couldn't blame him—he knew how he'd feel if Daisy were hurt. But he made no attempt to comfort the man or even speak to him. He had an idea any kind of conversation wouldn't be welcome at the moment. Instead, the two of them stood awkwardly together, side-by-side against the wall with their hands in their pockets.

Diane had done her best to make herself useful. She'd asked a lot of questions, but they seemed to be the right ones—Dr. Smith answered them patiently, even volunteered some information on exactly what she was doing to help Sugar. But it was fairly obvious that she viewed both of the visitors with some suspicion. If she'd asked more questions of her own—about where they were from, or what brought them to Mertonsville, or even the nature of their alleged friendship with Sam—that might have been less obvious. But she seemed to view them as an inconvenience better ignored.

"Will she be alright?" Diane asked, watching Carol carry the little dog out of the office, whispering gently to her.

"We'll know better tomorrow," Dr. Smith told her, sighing and pushing her fingers through her grey-streaked hair. "I think it could be worse. She has some broken bones and they may need more attention later. Right now, I need to go up and take a look at Sarge—sounds like he could be in much worse shape. Right, Sam?"

"Yeah," Sam said shortly, not looking up.

"You two don't need to come along," Smith said. Her manner was polite but firm—Josh had the idea that if Diane tried to push her, she might find she'd met her match. "Sarge is an old dog, and he's never been real friendly. He might not take well to strangers, especially if he's hurt.

"Besides, it's starting to get late, and there's not much to do after dark in Mertonsville. You should go back to your motel or wherever you're staying and get some rest. You can call in tomorrow, if you like, and Carol will give you an update."

Somewhat to Josh's surprise, Diane didn't argue. "Hope she gets better real soon," she told Sam, who shrugged and coughed and said, with his customary awkwardness—"Yeah, uh...thanks."

Despite the urgency in Smith's manner, neither Sam nor the doctor made a move to leave. It was fairly obvious they were waiting for them to go first, and Josh had no problem with that. Diane followed him slowly, with downcast eyes—for her, this was unwontedly docile behavior.

"Did you see her books?" she demanded, throwing an arm around him and more or less dragging him toward the car.

"What books? What are you talking about?"

"In her office, you goob! God, could you be any more oblivious? I saw them in just before we went into the examination room. The bookshelves are wall to wall books on primatology! I mean, a few other things, but mostly primates. Everything from Jane Goodall on up, and from about that era—the '70s and '80s, like that."

Josh sighed as he fished his keys out of his pocket. "And this is weird...why? I mean, she's a vet, right? Maybe she worked at a zoo or something one time. Or maybe she's just interested in monkeys. And as far as the age of the books...well, I hate to tell you, Diane, but the good doctor is maybe just a wee bit older than you and me...*ow*!"

Diane aimed another punch at his arm, before being distracted by a furiously affectionate Daisy, who promptly launched herself out the open door into her arms. "Oohh...oh my good girl! Who's all salty? My salty girl! Who had some French fries, huh? Who had her some yummy French fries?"

Josh groaned. "Oh God, she *did* get into the food! I can't catch a break tonight!"

"Man up, dude, you could stand to lose a few pounds. But Josh, those books...I'm telling you, something's up with this woman. Did you see how she reacted when I asked her about local Bigfoot sightings?"

"I didn't know you *did* ask her," Josh grumbled, picking desultorily through the ravaged burgers. Daisy, bless her heart, had left the buns and onion slices, but had eaten *all* the beef.

"I only got a chance to do it the one time, while we were waiting for the first set of X-rays. I did it real casual, you know. She gave me this look like...you know, if looks could kill? I mean, I wouldn't be here talking to you now."

"Yeah, how awful would *that* be?" Josh said, sliding behind the steering wheel. "Listen, can we stop and get something to replace Daisy's dinner? I'm starved."

"Not a bad idea," Diane said, shutting the door on her side. "They're obviously waiting for us to go. You notice they haven't followed us out yet? I saw a burger place down the road. Probably not as good as Dolly's, but we should have just enough time to grab you something before they come out and head out to Sam's. They won't even know we're following them."

Josh stared at her. "And we're doing that, *why*, exactly?"

Diane grinned at him, rubbing Daisy's ears. "I have a feeling Sam's place is the happening spot out here, cryptid-wise. And I have a feeling Sarge might not be a dog."

SIX

The road leading up to Sam's place wound through the last word in spooky forests. Ribbons of mist threaded between the jagged branches of trees still mostly leafless. Something about the forest looked inhospitable; downright *mean. Scooby Doo country*, Josh thought glumly. *I bet we pass the Mystery Machine. Maybe Shaggy'll spot me a burger from his stash.* They had reached the burger place Diane had seen just in time to witness the place closing for the night. *Small town living...gotta love it.*

Their car's headlights helped, but not much. Diane had insisted they forego the high beams, to help keep Sam from realizing he was being tailed. His battered station wagon stayed just visible in the gloom, far enough ahead to keep him in sight. Thing was, he was speeding big-time, really tearing up gravel, and Josh had to haul ass just to keep from losing him in one of the sharp turns. Diane had found a Sam Murowski on Pike on her phone and plugged the address into the GPS. That was fine for a back-up, but missing one of those turns would have been easy, leaving them backtracking in the darkness.

"How do people find their way around here?" Josh grumbled, swerving to miss a swift-footed something that darted in front of them and disappeared moments later into the forbidding woods.

"They're just used to it, is all," Diane said, picking through the shards of fried potato Daisy had left in the Styrofoam containers. "They probably don't go driving around these roads after dark, and if they do, they know every inch of 'em. It's the same back where I'm from. You think the Barrens are any picnic to drive in?"

Josh grunted, more interested in keeping from rolling the car.

"You think Sam really has a pet Bigfoot?" *Or gugwe*? *Or Chupacabra*? Or…

"He kinda looks like the type, wouldn't you say? But I'm more interested in whatever it was that managed to hurt it."

Josh nodded slowly. He hadn't actually thought about that.

Suddenly, the far-off gleam of Sam's tail lights disappeared, as they made a sudden left turn. "*Turn left on Pike Road, and arrive at destination in…three minutes*," the GPS droned.

"Don't turn yet," Diane said urgently, touching Josh's shoulder. "We don't want a confrontation. Just park on the side of the road up here."

Avoiding confrontations always made sense to Josh, but it brought up another question. "So what are we going to do?" he asked, pulling the car over. "Sit here all night?"

"Give them a minute to park and check on Sarge. Then we'll go up and see what the situation is."

Josh leaned back in his seat, sighing. After a time, he opened up the door.

"Bio break," he said. "Be right back."

Diane grunted, engrossed in her phone.

It was cool outside and smelled of damp greenery. *This would almost be peaceful, if it weren't so damned creepy*. Josh picked a likely spot and stood listening to the hissing of his pee in the dead leaves.

He was beginning to seriously miss his apartment back in New York, where you could get a pizza at any hour of the day or night. For that matter, he was starting to seriously wonder if the whole trip wasn't a mistake. On his own, he would have been on the road back home by now. But Diane was now deeply into her *Harriet the Spy* mode; she wouldn't be turned aside by something so trivial as anxiety and physical discomfort. Leaving her on her own didn't feel like an option, but he knew she wasn't going to leave until she'd resolved the mystery to her satisfaction. There were just too many leads, from the books in Dr. Smith's office to "Sarge" all the way down to the mysterious *gugwe* photos.

When he and Diane had first got together, the idea of teaming up and combining their individual skills had seemed so appealing. *But maybe it's just not meant to be.*

As he was pondering these things, a sudden breeze kicked up, blowing a smell into his face so foul he nearly gagged.

Holy heck, he thought, clapping a hand to his mouth and trying to keep from inhaling. *That's not me*. He might have been a lousy cryptozoologist by most standards, but even he knew what a sudden blast of swamp-stink in a deserted forest might portend.

"Diane," he said loudly, zipping hurriedly and turning back to the car. "I think we'd better..."

Three very large patches of darkness separated themselves from the surrounding shadow. One of them was standing over the car while its companions moved slowly toward Josh. Daisy was barking up a storm while Diane industriously cranked up the windows.

The things weren't ghosts; he could hear twigs snapping and gravel crunching under their outsized feet, heard a steady pant-pant-pant of their foul breath. More, the things exuded a physicality that made the hair on his neck stand up; he could all too easily imagine them grabbing him and shaking the life out of him.

"*Ten-hut*," the nearest creature grunted. He saw it was cradling something in its massive arms, a sticklike something it suddenly turned on Josh, raising it to its cheek and holding it for all the world like a rifle.

"*Te-en*-hut!" the thing snarled again, as though it found Josh's lack of response profoundly irritating.

Josh blinked, not quite able to believe what he'd heard. Was that "Ten-hut" as in a military command for attention? Did soldiers even use such an expression in the real world? He realized he had no idea. Then he heard a click sounding from the thing the *gugwe* was holding. It sounded uncomfortably like a rifle's safety being switched off. Its companion stepped back silently, the image of a lackey giving way to a superior.

Holy crap, I'm about to be executed by Sergeant Rock.

Something behind him squealed sharply. A second later, a sizable stone flew into the picture, striking the *gugwe* in the side of the head. The creature staggered backward, snarling.

"Josh!" Diane grabbed him from behind by one arm, pulling him back toward the car. "Get in, come on!" The door on the driver's side was hanging open. Something stood crouched behind it, writhing as though in enormous pain. Daisy stood on the seat, wagging her tail and barking furiously as her mistress dove inside.

Josh followed her. For a moment, they were a very unsexy tangle of arms and legs, and he was terrified he was going to feel a bullet bury itself in his ass. Then they somehow righted themselves and he had the door shut and locked, the key grinding in the ignition.

He could see two dark shapes advancing on the car as he struggled to start the engine, slowly lowering their rifles into position. A moment later, a third shadow slammed against the door on Diane's side, roaring. She screamed over Daisy's frantic barking, shoving up against him.

"Please tell me you didn't kick that thing in the balls?"

Diane snorted. "I had no idea men's sympathy for each others' genitals went so far. Will you *drive*, please? Before these things get the idea to shoot the windows out?"

"Too late," Diane groaned. Sure enough, Sgt. Rock had positioned himself directly in front of the car, raising his rifle again, eyes glowing as he took careful aim. *Damn, bubba, you really want to shoot that thing, don't you? And poor you, I'm not giving you the chance…*

At that moment, the car's much-put-upon engine finally turned over and Josh slammed his foot on the gas. They shot forward and hit Sgt. Rock with a satisfying jolt of impact. Josh shut his eyes as the car bumped ahead, trying not to think, trying not to hear the squeals.

Oh jeez, oh jeez, oh jeez…

"Get back to the highway!" Diane screamed.

That was when things really went to hell. Suddenly, *gugwe* were bursting out of the trees on both sides, screaming. Not all of them were armed, but the ones who were fired at the car indiscriminately. Luckily, most of the shots went wide, but one turned the windshield into a spiderweb of cracked glass.

Josh swerved wildly to avoid the mob of *gugwe* running at the car. If he hit them, they wouldn't just go down like Sgt. Rock had—they would all dogpile on the car and use the butts of their rifles to smash the windows in. Then it'd be game over for real.

It was chaos inside the car. Daisy was continuing to offer commentary from the back seat, so loudly and rapidly her barking had ceased to sound like any noise a dog might make. Diane was screaming and beating on the dashboard, less like a damsel in distress and more like an amazon furious at having been dumped into battle without a weapon. Josh didn't doubt she'd give a decent account of herself if the *gugwe* got at them. Himself, he was starting to think it might be nice to just shut his eyes and hope the end wouldn't be too painful.

"Turn left on Pike Road," the GPS suggested placidly. "You will arrive at your destination in…three…"

Josh seized on the suggestion, turning the car around in a frantic U-turn and driving up Pike as fast as the car would go. He heard shrieks and hoots from behind the car.

The bumpy road led them to a tall, ramshackle house with a single light burning in the downstairs window. He saw Sam's old station wagon parked nearby, but there was no other sign of anyone else who might be willing to aid them. And the road ended at the house. What he'd hoped would be an avenue for escape had turned out to be a one-way trap.

Josh leaned on the horn, blaring away as loud as he could. He could see a few *gugwe* hot-footing it away from the noise, but most of them were advancing on the parked car, rifles lowered.

That's when the roar came.

Josh's first thought was he'd never heard anything like it before. But even before Diane shouted "'Squatch! It's a 'Squatch!" he realized he had, many times. He'd heard it while sitting in his wonderfully safe and cozy home office munching chips and guzzling energy drinks and reaching for his laptop when Diane begged him to play that "Bigfoot calls" sound file just *one* more time…

But there was something there he'd never heard before, an intensity that just wouldn't come through a computer's speakers. Whatever was making this sound—loud and roaring, but with a whistling undercurrent—was *angry*.

A number of the *gugwe* now backed away from the car, their attention clearly taken up by something moving toward them in the darkness. Something like them, but even bigger, even more solid and dangerous-looking. It moved slowly, with a stop-start gait that suggested it wasn't doing so well, but it never stopped completely.

The *gugwe* screamed at it, some aiming their rifles. Others jumped the bigger creature, even as their fellows' guns went off. The *gugwe* clearly had no concept of waiting for a clean shot; several dropped to the ground, while others were flung down and unceremoniously stomped.

"We should help it," Diane whispered. By now, all the *gugwe* had moved away from the car, fully engaged with this new threat.

Josh turned incredulous eyes on her. "Help it *how*, exactly?"

"See how slowly it's moving?" Diane asked, lifting her hand to the windshield. She pressed a finger to the place on the glass, briefly blotting out the Bigfoot and slowly dragged it downward. Her voice was wondering and sad. "I think it's hurt. Remember, Sam told Dr. Smith the *gugwe* really tore it up before he chased them away?'"

Josh took a deep breath. No matter how cowardly it made him look, he had no intention of leaving the car or allowing Diane to. He had no illusions about the *gugwe* taking them prisoner, marching them at rifle-point back to their burrow or whatever. Even if they could fire guns, these were *animals*. His mind kept going back to the news story he'd seen of the woman in California who'd been savaged by a friend's pet chimp. *Forget shooting us.*

They could tear our faces off. Gouge out our eyes, eat our fucking hands.

But this was Diane, so you had to present it logically.

"Diane, it's a hell of a lot bigger than either those things or us. We have no idea how friendly it is, or if it *is* friendly. I thought you'd already bowed out of the whole Bigfoot-as-happy-nature-spirit camp."

But by now the *gugwe*-on-Bigfoot battle had pretty much started without them. Roars thundered outside the car, and screeches that deepened into those eerie, whale-like howls. Big as he was, Sarge was moving like a fury, picking *gugwe* off him like fleas and throwing them aside. Rifle-shots cracked repeatedly, and several times Sarge winced violently. After a relatively short time the shots stopped, but the *gugwe* apparently were well aware of how easily a rifle could be pressed into service as a club. Even Josh began to second-guess his decision to let discretion be the better part of valor. Sarge was *not* having an easy time of it. In short order, he was on his knees, fighting just to stay upright.

Then another shot rang out, and the *gugwe* turned their heads toward a second dark figure, much smaller than Sarge, that was striding toward them from the house. It raised its rifle and fired repeatedly, its shot much surer than theirs had been. Several *gugwe* fell and the others beat a hasty retreat.

Their savior touched Sarge briefly on the shoulder, as though to reassure himself he wasn't dead, then headed to the car.

A moment later, he was rapping on the window. Sam's broad, mean-looking face glowered at them through the glass. "Younse need to get in the house," he grated. "*Now*."

***

The Aladdin's Inn was the first place Jerry found on the road, and Marty, after a quick glance at the place, pronounced it suitable.

"Let's keep in touch," he told Jerry. "Especially if you hear from you-know-who."

Jerry grinned. "Don't worry. You'll be the first guy I call."

Half an hour later, Marty was toweling off after a quick shower. If the Aladdin wasn't remarkably less sleazy than some of the places he'd stayed, neither was it noticeably worse. At least you couldn't *see* the bedbugs scattering around the sheets. There were several fast-food places within walking distance, and what had looked like a liquor store, but he didn't feel like either eating or—for a wonder—drinking. He didn't dress, either. He'd been in his clothes all day and they still stank of the tire fire that had claimed Wilcox's facility. The fresh suit he'd brought was back in the conference room. Better to let the old one air out a little. He'd have get a cab out to the nearest shopping center the next day and get some casuals for the long trip to wherever he was going.

He sat down on the bed and switched on the local news. Unsurprisingly, there was nothing about an altercation at a nearby underground military establishment. Marty didn't doubt Wilcox's men had the local media well-trained to ignore anything unusual that might pop up on any given day.

He turned off the TV and eased back onto the bed, hands behind his head, thinking furiously about his escape plans. Booking tickets under his own name would probably be not so much stupid as suicidal. Luckily, he had a separate ID and credit card under an assumed name, with just enough funds to ensure a quick departure from just about anywhere in the continental USA. It had been an expensive insurance policy, and a risky one, but he was glad of it now.

He was more tired than he realized. He felt himself sinking into sleep and didn't resist it.

He woke up to his phone ringing. The ringtone was "Trouble Comin' Every Day" by the Mothers. Marty shut his eyes, indulging in a ten-second fantasy of some tropical island with sugar-white sand and a population of giggling young women who just adored mixing unhealthily potent cocktails for slightly overweight middle-aged men.

After two more serenades by the Mothers, he heard the ping of an incoming text. Sighing, he reached for his phone. "CALL ME" appeared in the text window, the letters small and hard and accusatory. It also said the time was 2:30 PM, CST.

You can't put this off forever, he thought. If he was lucky, this might actually be the first step to cutting Wilcox's apron-strings forever.

Of course, he'd never been a remarkably lucky man.

"Hi, Dad," he said brightly.

Whoever was on the other end didn't sound so good. Their breathing was ragged and congested-sounding. For a brief moment, he actually doubted his caller was Wilcox.

"Hey, baby," Marty deadpanned. "What are you wearing?"

"Cowardly sack of shit," the voice grated. *Oh, yeah, that's him. That's the boy.*

"And I was supposed to do…what? Grab a pencil and stand valiantly by your side with 'The Star-Spangled Banner' playing in the background, hoping to jab it one of those things' butts before it tore my throat out?"

"You were engaged…" Wilcox swallowed suddenly before a long moment of silence. *That's right, I was engaged in saving my ass.*

"You were engaged by your country to perform a service," Wilcox said finally. "You…"

"Where are you, Tom?" Marty asked, a little more gently. The old man didn't sound too good.

Wilcox gave a snort of laughter. "Where you think? Private room in Mt. Sinai? I'm back here at the facility, needledick. Meds patched me up. They tell me it wasn't as bad as it looks. Had three of those bastards hanging off me. The *teeth* on those things, Christ…"

Marty shut his eyes. "So why are you calling?" *They've got him on something, it sounds like. If there's a reason for this call, I'd better get it out of him ASAP before he zones out.*

Wilcox chuckled. Marty could see the old man lying in a hospital bed, covered in bloody bandages. "Always get right to the point, eh, Bloom?"

"First thing they teach you in journalism school. Look, Tom, you were never remarkably straight with me or any of your 'skeptics.' If you were, you wouldn't have had us running away when your little *kaffeeklatsch* suddenly turned into a creature feature. What were those things, Tom? They weren't your garden variety Sasquatch. Closer to Rolandson's *gugwe*, but even nastier. Were they the ones who smoked us out of the facility? They were armed, for chrissakes, so I would think they could handle a simple tire-fire."

"That's classified, Bloom." *Alright, li'l Tommy doesn't wanna play nice, so it's time to wrap this up*, Marty thought.

"Okay, I'm being straight with *you* now. I'm not coming back. That's firm, General. Make me disappear if you can. You'll have to find me first. We both know that won't be easy."

A silence followed, punctuated by a hacking cough. Marty was on the point of hanging up, when Wilcox said, "Then do one thing for me."

"What?" Marty's voice was cautious.

"I'll tear up your paperwork, that's what you want. Nobody'll bother you. No men in black showing up at your house. I'll even authorize a very healthy severance package for you, and don't bother with the 'I don't care about the money,' bullshit. I know you better.

"But I do need you to do me this one service. And this is off the clock, Marty. Uncle Sam doesn't know. I need you to find a civilian for me, and deliver something to her. I could get someone else, but it'd take longer, and even though I can barely believe I'm saying this, it would ultimately be an even bigger pain in the ass than dealing with you. This civilian has her picture in the dictionary under 'paranoid.' Holed up in some shit-town in PA. She won't trust anybody has even the slightest whiff of the military on 'em, so you're perfect."

"*Her*? Who we talking about, that Jane Goodall wannabe from your PowerPoint deck?"

Tom chuckled. "Never any flies on your shit, were there, Bloom?" His chuckle devolved into a nasty-sounding hacking. "You got a pencil? We'd better do this fast, the nurse is coming for my 0-eleven check-in and let me tell you, he is a real ball-breaker."

SEVEN

Sam wouldn't let them stop for a decent look at Sarge. Diane wanted to. She stood staring at the damaged 'Squatch. He looked back at her, growling deep in his throat—it didn't sound like a threat so much as a warning to stay back. Josh thought the signals were pretty obvious; they were what you might get from any injured animal. *I'm hurt. I'm not right. Leave me alone.*

Diane reached for her pocket and Sam slapped the barrel of his rifle against her side—not hard enough to be overly threatening or even insulting, but hard enough to demand attention.

"Get up the house," he said, nodding at the structure further up the yard.

"I was just going to use the light," she said, sounding hurt. "Get a better look at him, see if I can…aw, come on, man, I've been looking for this my *whole life*."

"Get up the house," Sam snapped. His voice was hard and pissed off. "Go on."

Josh followed numbly. Daisy was on her lead, practically glued to his ankles. The air still reeked of *gugwe*. Even Josh could smell it; he didn't blame the dog for not liking it. The ground was littered with hairy bodies. He wondered what Sam was going to do with them. Burn them? Bury them?

They passed Dr. Smith, striding purposefully down from the house with her medical bag. She didn't look at them, but said, "Hell of a night," in passing.

"Let me help," Diane begged, but the vet didn't answer, and Diane, for once, didn't push it.

Inside, Sam's house was as messy as Josh would have expected, with a stale smell, but there were signs someone else had lived there once. There were folksy knick-knacks and framed photographs everywhere, all covered with thick coats of dust. Many of the photographs showed a boy posing with various dead animals, squinting into the camera—undoubtedly a much younger version of Sam. A few showed a tall, balding man Josh assumed was his father. A single picture showed a worn-looking woman standing by young Sam, her face fierce with pride.

I'm guessing his mom did the decorating. Sam probably didn't change a single thing once they passed away.

Daisy found two stainless steel bowls on the floor. The one that Josh assumed was meant for food was empty. The other was half full of water, and Daisy set about emptying it. Sam didn't seem to mind.

"Why'd you follow us?" Sam asked. Josh noticed he didn't put the rifle down, though he wasn't pointing it at them.

"We wanted to help," Diane said, her hands outstretched appealingly.

"Younse wanted to *snoop*," Sam said, his face coloring in a way that made his views on snooping very clear. "The screamers saw you and came back. They might've left us alone, but when they smelled you, they had to come back. They know you're not from up here. You shouldn't have come back."

"Well, *you* weren't honest with us," Diane said, cheeks coloring as her fight coming back. "We asked you if you knew anything about local Bigfoot sightings, and you were all like, '*bluh-bluh-bluh-duuh*!'" She rolled up her eyes and waved her hands around spastically.

"What the hell is *that* supposed to be?" Josh demanded. If he thought the sarcasm in his voice would bring Diane back to her senses, he was dead wrong.

"That was *him*! 'Aww, shucks, I dunno, I dunno nothin', duhh, I don't know what ta do with someone's business card, I'm just a good ol' boy, huh-huh-huh!'"

Josh glanced at Sam, terrified he was getting ready to club her to death with his rifle. Instead, he was staring at her gesturings with a strange, cold fascination that said, clear as day, *So this is what a crazy person is like*. It was a look he'd seen before on other people when Diane really got going.

"I think younse both better get in the basement," he said, gesturing with his rifle at a small door in the wall between the kitchen and dining room. "Go on, now. Dr. Smith said she'd talk to you later."

"No!" Diane cried, her shoulders lowering. "Please, man, look, I'm sorry…I'm just frustrated. Don't you realize, you could like be famous! You're sitting right on top of a mystery people have been trying to solve for over a century! Two centuries! *We've* been looking for it all our lives!"

"I don't know nothing about any of that," Sam said stolidly. "I told you, Dr. Smith'll talk to you. Go on, now."

"C'mon, Diane," Josh said, tugging gently at her arm. "He's not going to talk to you."

Diane must have seen the sense in that. She whistled for Daisy, but the dog had already settled herself in the living room on Sam's couch.

"Traitor," she said darkly. "Let's go, girl, come on."

Sam went into the living room. Josh tightened up nervously, but when he came back, he had Daisy in his arms—the rifle, Josh noticed, he'd left behind on the couch. Whether this was meant as a half-assed olive branch, Josh wasn't sure. But he was glad of it, nonetheless.

"Here you go," Sam said. He sure wasn't smiling, but he was gentle enough handing Daisy over to Diane. A few minutes later, he opened up the cellar door and the two went downstairs to their exile.

The cellar of Sam's house felt like a dungeon chamber right out of a horror comic—cold and drafty, with a pervasive smell of damp earth. As Josh went down the stairs, he trailed his hand against the wall, feeling uneven blocks of stone mortared roughly together—probably decades ago. Things looked a little better when he turned on the light. It was pretty rough, but they found no skeletons chained to the walls. Instead, there was a reasonably new furnace and water heater in one corner, as well as piles of crates and boxes Josh guessed Sam kept here for want of any other storage space. The rear of the basement was mostly shadow, with more boxes piled up in the gloom, but just before that section he could see a toilet, and even a refrigerator that when opened proved to be full of beer. *Welcome to Pennsylvania,* he thought wryly.

Diane helped herself to a can, popping the top and drinking down half at a swallow. "Thirsty," she muttered, by way of explanation.

"You sure that's a good idea?"

Diane belched behind her hand. "Come on, Josh, this guy's not some kind of ogre. I don't think he's going to begrudge me a lousy beer."

"Maybe he's not an ogre, but he locked us in his castle pretty quick," Josh pointed out.

"Yeah, well, he didn't do a very good job," Diane said, taking her phone out of her pocket and wagging it at him. "He should have taken these. We could call for help anytime we want to."

"So let's do it."

Diane snorted. "Like who? The National Guard? The Anti-Evil Bigfoot Squad? Besides, Sam said Dr. Smith was coming to talk to us. I think that's worth waiting for." She strolled around the room, sipping her beer and humming tunelessly. Josh recognized this as her thinking mode. Sighing, he sat down to wait.

Suddenly, Daisy, who had been happily subjecting everything in nose-range to a thorough sniffing, darted past her mistress into the darkened end of the cellar. A moment later, the basement was ringing with her angry barks.

Diane reached up and pulled a string from the ceiling, bathing the entire room in light.

"What's *that*?"

"That" was a large canvas tarpaulin that had been folded roughly up and shoved against a stack of boxes. Had Diane not pointed it out, Josh probably wouldn't have noticed it. Suddenly, it looked very conspicuous—mostly for the dark stains that were almost certainly blood. Another stack nearby it proved to be a set of three worn, heavy books that looked like bank ledgers.

Now that they were back here, there was a smell in this corner of the basement that made Josh feel sick to his stomach. It had certainly attracted Daisy, who was running in circles around the folded tarpaulin, alternatively sniffing at it and barking wildly. The smell made him less than eager to unfold the tarpaulin, but he pulled it into the light and saw coarse grey hairs stuck to the half-dried batches of blood. He pinched up samples of these and tucked them into his pocket, wishing he had a baggie to hold them.

Diane, meanwhile, was busily inspecting the books, flipping through the pages with an intent expression.

"Ohmigod. Josh, look at this!"

"What is it? The *Necronomicon*?" He walked over and glanced over Diane's shoulder. A moment later, he wished he'd had a beer first.

The ledger's pages were old and much stained with something that the years had turned brown. They were covered with drawings and sketches, every spare inch of space filled up with notes written in a tiny, almost unreadable hand. Other pages were devoted entirely to those relentless, unreadable notes.

The drawings themselves all showed apes or apelike creatures of various kinds. The earlier pages in the book contained fairly conventional portraits of gorillas, orangutans, and chimps that might have been done in the primate house at any zoo. But as Diane continued turning pages, the images became steadily stranger. The earliest of these showed what were recognizably supposed to be Sasquatch. Others were chimp-like beings that brought back memories of documentaries Josh had seen on *Australopithecus*. But even these were steadily displaced by stranger creatures with human-like bodies, pronounced snouts with savage-looking tusks, and those staring eyes—*gugwe*. One particularly disturbing picture—which Josh was sure would haunt him until the day he died—showed a weird, stooped critter like a huge-eyed tarsier halfway evolved into a human form.

Some of the pictures were in charcoal and pencil. Some were in ballpoint pen, the point pressed so firmly into the paper that in places it had almost torn through. Most showed the animals in naturalistic poses. Others were anatomical studies, showing details of muscle and bone structure. All of them displayed not just talent but a strange obsessiveness—whoever had done them was focused utterly on capturing the animals, as though the opportunity might be snatched away at any moment.

There was also a thin sheaf of photos—Polaroids and a couple prints that had been blown up from a smaller size. These showed a much younger Dr. Smith interacting with what could only be a young *gugwe*. One photo showed her holding up flashcards, the kind used to teach basics of grammar and arithmetic to small children, while the *gugwe* looked on. In others, she looked on while the *gugwe* frolicked on a set of monkey-bars in what looked like an outdoor prison yard. The last one was a close-up of a human hand—Dr. Smith's, apparently, manipulating the digits of the *gugwe*'s hairy paw. At first, Josh had no idea what he was looking at. Then it struck him—*that's sign. She's teaching it sign language.*

"So what do you make of all this? 'Cause I'm not getting a whole lot."

"She was working with some kind of experiment to breed a new kind of animal based at least partially on cryptid stock," Diane said, her eyes gleaming. "My guess is that it was something to do with the military. And that *gugwe* she's with in those photos must have been her star pupil."

Josh turned one of the photographs over. On the back were the words *Caliban—1981, August, initial lang. exp.*, written in faded pencil. Next he turned back to the book's scribble-covered pages. There was no question the handwriting on the photo matched that in the journals, though it was far more legible.

"I can't read most of the writing in the book. She might have used a code or something. Every now and then you can just make out something in Latin—scientific names for the animals, I guess, but there's something in this part over here that's really disturbing." She pointed at a line of text with one finger. "See?"

"*Ebola*?" Josh asked, eyes widening as he puzzled out the letters. Three question marks followed the words.

"Yeah. I don't know if she's speculating on how Ebola might affect the different species or what. And there are other names here that sound like other diseases, but I'm not so sure about them." She shook her head. "Now I almost wish I hadn't opened it."

"You and me both," Josh murmured. "Why do you think she brought these books out here to Sam's? Nothing against the guy, but he doesn't strike me as much of a reader."

"For reference, probably. See all the stuff about anatomy? I think she must have had Sarge laid out on that tarpaulin and was using 'Squatch sections while she worked on him. These books probably represent most of the knowledge she's amassed during her entire career, Josh. Her whole *life*."

"So if she knows all this about apes and every kind of ape-flavored cryptid in existence, what's she doing playing animal doctor out here in Pennsylvania?"

"Beats me. But it makes me all the more interested in talking to her." Diane looked at the ceiling as she finished off her beer, as though waiting for Dr. Smith's footsteps to sound above them.

"Here. Help me."

"Doing what?"

"I need you to hold the books open," Diane said, thrusting the ledger into his arms. "We have a contact, remember? The guy who told us about the *indri* calls? I want him to see this stuff."

Josh didn't make his usual protests about how maybe Dr. Smith wouldn't want to share her research with outsiders. This was bigger than that. He knelt down and used bricks from a pile in the corner to weigh the pages down while Diane took pictures of them with her phone. It was a long process, but that was alright. *I don't think we're in any hurry, here*, he thought.

***

Joyce Kovacs—aka Dr. Joyce Smith—stared down wearily at Sarge, or what was left of him. The first pack of *gugwe* had torn him up badly—the second bunch had seemingly been determined to finish the job. She could tell from his pale gums he'd lost a great deal of blood. She could see it shining blackly in the grass around him.

She just shut her eyes for a moment, gathering her strength.

"Alright, big fella. Let me take a look at you." She had built up Sarge's trust in her over a period of years, nearly as long as she'd known Sam. She knew Sarge didn't particularly like her—he was a mean old bastard, like most of the big males who lived long enough. Why he and Sam tolerated each other was a mystery, but she was grateful for it. Sarge could see Sam trusted her, and that was enough for him, though he kept looking at her with his beady little eyes like he suspected she was going to try and rip his hairy balls off.

She took the pistol out from under her coat. Sarge knew what it was—he could see it and no doubt smell it—and he had watched

Sam shoot enough times that he knew what it was for. He bared his fangs at her, but he was too weak to take a swipe at her.

She made it fast and hopefully painless, aiming right between his eyes. The pistol's crack echoed in the trees and somewhere at one Sam's neighbors a dog started up barking. Sam would hear it too, she knew, and he wouldn't like it. Couldn't blame him—she wasn't entirely sure he considered her a friend, and she'd just deep-sixed the only real one he had, apart from poor Sugar.

But she couldn't help it. She slipped the gun back in her pocket and took out her phone.

One more thing to do before Sam came out, and she could already hear him, tramping swiftly toward her, calling "Dr. Smith? Hey—Dr. Smith!" She made the call quickly.

"Ricky? Yeah, you know who this is. We got a lot of 'em out here. You're going to have to move fast."

They knew her in Bernswood. Ricky sure did. She'd helped him get through school and make it as a vet assistant at a time when his future seemed mostly about cooking meth. He and his wife had just had a little girl and bought their first house—he had no particular interest in cryptids.

The animal hospital there was a lot bigger than her little practice, with resources they'd never heard of in Mertonsville. They had a crematorium, for instance. A big one, that could be used to take care of deer killed by drunk drivers as well as dead strays. By the time the sun came up over the mountains, the dead *gugwe* and poor old Sarge would be ashes. There'd likely be some very interesting remains left in the grass of Sam's yard if anyone really wanted to look, but Dr. Julie Kovacs seriously doubted anyone would.

She could hear Sam running now, shouting at her. She shut her eyes and turned to face him. This wasn't going to be easy.

EIGHT

Josh woke up with a sudden start at the sound of Diane's phone. He had fallen asleep, embarrassingly enough, perched on the toilet. It had been the most convenient place to sit, and he hadn't wanted to lie down on the cold floor, as Diane had. At least she had Daisy curled up next to her, and a blanket from one of the storage boxes.

By the time he had walked over to her, Diane had picked up the call. Josh checked his own phone and was surprised to see it was late morning. Sam hadn't come to let them out and there had been no sign during the night of Dr. Smith.

Diane was wearing her "amazed" look as she traded jabbers with whoever was on the other end. She paced rapidly from one end of the room to the other.

"Okay," she said suddenly. "Okay, just, wait…I'm putting you on speaker." She glanced at Josh with wide, frightened eyes. "Could you repeat what you just told me?" she asked. "I've got my boyfriend Josh on the line."

"Hi, Josh," a British-accented voice said from the speaker. He sounded friendly, and, paradoxically, scared shitless at the same time. "This is Randall Hutchins down at the Primate Resource Center in Sydney. I traded messages with you and your charming girlfriend yesterday about some sound files of what sounded like *indri* calls…"

"Yeah," Josh said, unsure of how he felt about the "charming girlfriend" remark. "So, uh…we're sort of trapped in a basement up here in Pennsylvania? And we…"

"Will you stop being a jealous ass," Diane hissed, punching his arm. "You know they all have lousy teeth!"

"Sorry, Diane, didn't quite catch that?"

"Kkkkhhhh," Diane said, making electronic hissing sounds into the phone. "Sorry, Randall, you were breaking up a little. Just go on."

"Anyway, your Diane is just a goldmine of fascinating information! She just sent me some absolutely mind-boggling photographs of pages from someone's journals. Absolutely incredible, like something from my wildest fantasies…"

"Eeuw," Josh whispered, making a face. Diane punched him again.

"It took me some time to really make out the text. It's *not* a code, as Diane thought, it's just written very, very small…and it's basically this person engaged in a kind of written conversation with herself. Listen…

"'Not much doubt of it now, the others are all showing signs of infection, as does C.' Not sure who C. is, of course. Probably one of her test subjects. 'Individuals react differently, the males more quickly than the fem.' I assume that's short for females. Anyway, there's a great deal of technical stuff, but putting it all together, it's obvious that whoever wrote these journals was involved in an experiment not only in genetic engineering, creating an entirely new species of primate unlike anything that's ever been in the world, but also engineering a disease capable of destroying them. It seems to be something that attacks their auto-immune capabilities. I mean, really destroys them. At first, it seems like your standard garden-variety supervirus. It sickens them, and then…well, they sort of disintegrate at a cellular level. If I'm reading it correctly, you understand."

"But why?" Diane asked urgently. "I mean, why was she doing this? And for who? She couldn't have done it herself, someone was paying for the research. Did you get any hint of that?"

"Hate to tell tales out of school, love, but the bad guys here seem to be your own military. As far as why, I can only speculate. The writer doesn't really go into details, but I'd assume they knew exactly how dangerous these creatures could be, and so wanted something as a kind of insurance policy, as it were. I mean, you've got to tell me, where have you been getting all this fantastic stuff?"

"Listen, Randall," Diane said, ignoring the question. "Here's the big one. The disease she was working on…is it contagious? To humans, I mean?"

"Hmn? What? Oh, yes! Oh, if I'm reading this correctly, it's *terribly* contagious. The 'jump off' factor…that is, the ability of humans to catch it from a primate, is very high. Catch it just by looking at one of the beasties. Now, I hate to press you, love, but…"

Diane shut her phone up and let her hand drop to her side, staring off into the corner.

"So that's it," Josh said numbly.

"That's it," she replied, smiling tightly. "We've been exposed to whatever disease these things had. So has Sam, Dr. Smith…we're all going to die."

***

Wilcox had one of his goons waiting for him when he landed in Pittsburgh, all ready to make the drop-off. The guy snapped Marty a sharp salute as he handed off the package, and Marty returned it with a straight face. Several oldsters in the crowd turned all beaming and teary-eyed at the sight of the fat little guy in the Wisconsin Badgers sweatshirt saluting the tall soldier in the red beret. Did everything but come up and thank them for their service. Hell, no skin off Marty's ass. If it meant getting General Tom off his back permanently, he would have happily joined the guy in a duet of "Moon River," right there by the place that sold giant pretzels.

Marty waited 'til he got in his rental car (already paid for and waiting, courtesy of Wilcox) before he opened up the package, using the little pen-knife on his keychain. It contained a small, snub-nosed pistol-like dealy—looked kind of like the toy laser-guns Marty used to send off box-tops for when he was a kid. It was fitted with a gleaming metal cylinder and came with three other cylinders just like it, all set into the foam casing inside the package.

He could hear Wilcox's voice snarling in his inner ear. *That thing represents hundreds of thousands of dollars of taxpayers' money, Bloom. Don't get careless with it. Above all else, do not* lose *it.*

Awesome, dude. Marty had no intention of even *looking* at the thing again, if he could help it. He bundled the package closed and pushed it into the little canvas carry-all he'd bought back in Madison, then fired up the little Subaru Uncle Sam had rented him and got on his way.

He was in Mertonsville two hours later. The town was reasonably close to the mall where he'd done his last—and hopefully it would be his last—bookstore event. But if he'd thought the mall represented the last bastion of small-town America, he had another thing coming.

Mertonsville proper consisted of a single main street with several smaller streets branching off it. Local business consisted of a filling station with a sign out front announcing it didn't take debit cards, a candy store that looked like it hadn't had a visitor in ten years, and a restaurant called Dolly's.

There was no one on the streets. Not a single person. A head in the window at Dolly's peered at Marty as he drove by, but disappeared immediately as he turned to check the place out.

Thing was, it had been a while since the cup of coffee and stale croissant that represented the airline's idea of breakfast. Marty was hungry, and he needed someplace to serve as home base during this little adventure, should Dr. Julie Kovacs, aka Smith, not want to be found.

And despite Wilcox's assurances to the contrary, Marty's natural cynicism told him the latter was a real possibility. He had been trying to reach her since that morning, using the numbers Wilcox had given him. He had expected to at least have some luck at her office, but each time he dialed, he got zip. Not even an answering machine. Just a recorded message saying the number was out of order. That struck him as slightly worrying.

A few minutes later, Marty was seated in Dolly's with a large mug of thankfully strong coffee and a menu. "So what's good here?" Marty smiled. The coffee made him feel quite a bit friendlier.

The waitress blinked. Marty couldn't tell if she'd been the head eyeballing him through the window or not. "People like the burgers."

"That sounds good," Marty said, handing back the menu. "Hey, do you know a Dr. Julie Smith? She's the vet around here, I understand."

"Her office is up the hill, on Grant Avenue," the waitress told him. "She normally comes in mornings for her coffee, but I hain't seen her yet." She blinked again. "You need her for something?" It took Marty a moment to realize she was trying to make sense of his interest in Dr. Smith given a) his stranger status and b) his lack of any visible animal companion. The only other diner visible was an older man with an ancient dog of mixed provenance slumbering under his table.

“We’re old friends,” Marty said smoothly. “I happened to be in the area and I wanted to say hi.” Anywhere else, such a transparent lie probably would have raised suspicions, but the waitress only nodded and went to see about a burger for her new customer.

So if the good doctor is in any kind of trouble, the folks here in town are unaware of it. That might not say much, but unless she’s particularly close friends with any of the locals, it’s all I’ve got to go on.

After finishing his surprisingly tasty lunch, Marty headed up to Grant Street. It was some distance from Main Street, an isolated cinderblock building with a larger wing in the rear. There were no signs he could see out front indicating that this was vet’s office.

The door, however, was yawning wide open. There could be all sorts of non-worrying reasons for that, but right now Marty couldn’t think of a single one. He parked and walked cautiously up to the door, wishing like hell he’d hit Wilcox up for something to shoot with besides the little laser pistol or whatever it was.

The inside of the building was divided into a small waiting area, an equally small examination room and what Marty guessed was the doctor’s own office. The entire place was a wreck. Someone had apparently been very angry at Dr. Smith—from the smell, someone with serious digestive as well as mental problems. They had smeared the evidence of this all over the walls, hurling handful as well. Marty had to go outside and have a good gag before returning with his hand clamped over his nose. If he hadn’t felt the need to look for Smith, he would have been halfway down the highway by now.

Books, papers, and files lay scattered in torn, partially chewed masses on the floor, along with a laptop, smashed glassware, bottles of meds, a microscope, and various medical equipment, all of which had been slammed repeatedly onto the floor until they bore little resemblance to what they had been. Every chart and poster and piece of framed artwork on the walls had been torn down and smashed or torn.

At the rear of the examination room was a door leading into a small kennel—the outbuilding he'd seen from outside. Marty guessed this was where patients were kept. At the very back of the kennel, one of the doors stood open and something tall and hairy was stopped over something hairy and still. It was tearing at it with its fists and mouth, making wet noises.

Marty felt his stomach turning over. The creature was one of the same breed that had torn up Wilcox's facility back in Wisconsin. This had found its way into Smith's office—probably in the company of several others. What happened to its friends Marty had no idea, but this one had found the kennel and decided to stick around for lunch.

Something barked at him and he started. A small dog was staring at him from the kennel nearest his right side. The dog was apparently recuperating from some kind of treatment—it was lying on one side, its body wrapped in bandages. It didn't seem to like the smell of the intruder any more than Marty himself; it wriggled violently, trying to right itself.

"Shh," Marty whispered, slowly backing away and making calming motions with both hands. The *gugwe* hadn't yet heard him, probably too busy chowing down on the small dog's larger and less fortunate compatriot. But Marty's luck wasn't going to hold out forever…neither was the dog's, if he left it behind. It looked just about the right size to serve as the *gugwe*'s dessert.

I must be crazy, he thought. But he began opening the small dog's kennel. He could grab it and run like hell. The kennel door opened with a low screech of poorly lubricated hinges.

That did it. The dog jumped to its feet and began a rapid-fire barking assault on Marty's ears. Suddenly, the *gugwe* was on its feet, its red-smeared face staring balefully over its shoulder at Marty.

"Shit! Shitshit*shit*!" Marty grabbed the dog and thrust it whining under his arm. *If I live, I'll call you "Loudmouth,"* he thought at the dog. Then he ran with all the speed he could muster, the howling *gugwe* only a few feet behind him.

He tore through the office and nearly tripped over a small, dark-haired woman who was standing with a ripped book in either hand, looking at the wreckage with a hopeless expression.

"Move!" Marty screamed. She moved—thankfully, she had left the front door open and didn't shut it behind her when she made her own escape. Marty shambled out, hurrying toward his car. The girl was already in her own and was firing the ignition. Marty was tempted to get in shotgun and scream "Drive, damnit!" but he'd left Wilcox's package in his own car. That was just enough incentive for him to head for the rental.

The *gugwe* lunged out of the door behind him. He felt a slight breeze as its paw slashed at air behind him. He tore the rental's door open and tumbled the yelping dog in. Glancing behind him, he could see the thing was carrying a dilapidated rifle by the stock, the barrel dragging in the dirt. It either didn't really know what the rifle was for, or didn't think carrying it in a particular way mattered. It was already lifting it over its head, its red-stained jaws opening wide as it prepared to smash him over the noggin with it.

Marty remembered the scene back at the Madison facility, the weird way the *gugwe* and the soldiers seemed to interact.

It gave him an idea.

"At ease!" he screamed, putting everything he had in it, every drill he'd attended, every sergeant he'd ever either reluctantly respected or violently hated. The *gugwe* froze instantly, blinking at him with its bulging red eyes. It hissed, making an odd, wavering pass with the rifle, as though hoping this would somehow serve to magically kill the mouthy little human. It didn't, but neither did the *gugwe* take another step.

"At ease, soldier!" Marty snapped. He was easing himself into the car, silently willing the little dog to stop barking—which didn't really seem likely to happen. The young woman had pulled partway out of the parking lot and sat with the engine idling, watching with frightened, cautious eyes.

Incredibly, the *gugwe* raised its shoulders. "Ten-*hut*!" the creature grunted, as though this constituted a correct response. Marty blinked unbelievingly at it. It was all he could do not to break down in hysterical laughter.

"At ease!" Marty said again, pulling the rental's key out of his sweatpants and inserting it in the ignition. He was perfectly contented to keep up this charade as long as the creature wanted—or as long as it took him to get the hell out of Dodge.

A moment or two later, the rental eased out onto the driveway, back toward the main highway. The girl followed close behind, signaling him to pull over. After a quick glance in the rearview to ensure the *gugwe* wasn't chasing them, Marty did. The girl lowered her window and leaned out.

"That's Sugar," she said. For a moment, the words made absolutely no sense to Marty. The second time she said them, a bit more insistently, it felt like something from a dream.

"The dog!" she said, eyes glinting in exasperation. "Her name is Sugar, she belongs to one of the doctor's clients."

Marty had to admire the girl's spunk. She had just narrowly escaped having her face torn off from something from a cryptozoologist's wet dream, but all she could think about was doing right by her boss's clients.

Welcome to small-town America, he thought. "Okay, take her," he said. Sugar seemed a little the worse for the energy she had expended, but thumped her tail feebly as he handed her to the girl through the window. "Do you know where Dr. Smith is?" he asked. "I really need to find her. It has to do with those things...the ones that trashed her office."

"You didn't see her...back there, right?" she asked. Marty knew she was asking if he'd found her boss's body, and for once he was pleased to be able to shake his head.

"She might be at home, then. Or she might be at Sam's. She went with him last night after he dropped Sugar off. He said his other dog, Sarge, had been attacked by something, but…" her voice trailed off. "I don't think he really has another dog," she said confidentially. "I think Sarge is something else."

"So how about you check at her place? If you can give me this Sam guy's address, I'll put it in my GPS and I'll head out there." After a moment of consideration, she began reeling off an address that was probably only fifteen minutes away.

"Good enough," he said. "And listen…if you don't find the doctor at home, call the cops, right away." He didn't particularly want Mertonsville's finest involved in this game, but he knew it might ease the girl's mind if he was the one telling her to call the police. His thought was confirmed when the girl gave him a sober nod and pulled back onto the highway.

Besides, he thought grimly, putting the rental back into DRIVE, *I might need a little saving myself in an hour or so.*

NINE

Sam sat on the stump of an oak tree his father had cut down when he was eight. He couldn't remember why the old man had cut the old tree down; he'd just had one of his fits and, after his morning bourbon, taken off after it with his axe. His mother had started washing dishes, her usual method of dealing with his father's fits. There had been no dishes in the sink, so she'd simply taken clean ones out of the cabinet and washed those. Kept her busy all morning.

"Should've buried him," Sam said glumly, watching the truck rumble off, back to the crematorium at Bernswood.

"Be reasonable, Sam," Dr. Smith said. "If anyone found his body, this entire area would be taken over by the military. The state itself would change overnight."

"Yeah, but that guy who picked Sarge up…and the screamers…he ain't gonna get sick? Like whatsisname did?"

Dr. Smith rolled her eyes. Overall, she had a fairly high opinion of Sam's intellect, but like most people up here, he tended to latch onto ideas and not want to let go, especially those involving illness. She wouldn't have called Sam a hypochondriac, but he had a deep respect for what disease could do. After the career she'd had with Wilcox's team, she could hardly blame him.

"Caliban," she said quietly. *Not "whatshisname," for God's sake.*

"Caliban," Sam said respectfully, pronouncing it more like "Calben."

"I told you, the disease doesn't transfer to human hosts. Even if it had successfully infected the others, that was never the plan, for obvious reasons. Ricky's in no danger, any more than you or I."

"He told me he has a little girl, though."

"She's safe as houses. So is his wife. Look, if it makes you feel better, I'll keep an eye on him. The first sign of him getting anything more than sniffles, I'll get on the horn and have him airlifted to the Mayo Clinic."

Sam looked impressed. "You can do that?"

The expression on her face wasn't quite a smile. "I'd like to see anyone try and stop me."

Her phone rang in her pocket. She ignored it. Damned thing had been ringing all morning.

"So what now? I mean, I still got those kids in my cellar."

"That is concerning." She kept her eyes on the row of trees that fringed Sam's yard. She could see small shapes coming closer.

Some were moving in the treetops. Others crept along underneath, some holding rifles.

"I don't think it'll be a problem, though," she said, almost dreamily. "These things have a way of working themselves out."

Sam's eyes followed hers. A moment later, he was on his feet, panic resonating in his big frame. "Aw shit! Where the hell they coming from?"

"The woods. They belong here now, Sam, just like the black bear and the few members of Sarge's people that are left. You might as well put that rifle away, unless you have some shells stashed in your pocket. You've pretty much blown whatever ammo you already had."

She could see from his face that he knew she was right. He knew it but wasn't quite ready to come to terms with it yet. His eyes were frightened, and he kept shifting his weight from one foot to the other, like he needed to take a piss.

"You know what an invasive species is, Sam?"

Something in her voice made him calm down. Plus, Sam liked the shows on Animal Planet. "It's…it's animal that comes into a place and kinda takes over. Pushes out the animals that actually came from there."

Dr. Smith nodded gravely. "That's exactly right. Like rabbits did in Australia. The screamers, as you call them, have started doing that here. Up to now, the bulk of their population has been centered in the Midwest. You watch some of these cryptid shows, you'll hear them talk about 'dogmen' out in Wisconsin. Or *gugwe*. Like Bigfoot, but with snouts. After this is over, my guess is that most of them will go back there. Not all of them, though. They'll get a little foothold out here. Lots of territory to move into. Plenty of resources we're too stupid to have ever completely destroyed. Once they survive a few of our winters, they'll find it suits them just fine. And just like those Australian rabbits forced out the numbats and bandicoots, the *gugwe* will force out the native predators. And us. Oh, it'll take time. But as I say, these things have a way of resolving themselves."

"But why? Why'd they come here, if they were all out west?"

"Because they were looking for someone." She smiled a little.

Well, we've all got our monsters. Sam had Sarge, I have a bum named Caliban.

"S'cuse me, Sam. I have some people to talk to." She started walking toward the approaching *gugwe*. Sam watched her go, his mouth open. A moment later, he was running back toward the house.

***

Sam burst into the cellar through the back door. He stopped and stared in confusion at Diane and Josh, who sat with handkerchiefs clapped to her mouth. Diane stood up, backing toward the rear the cellar, waving him away one-handed. Daisy ran around in circles, barking happily.

"Stay back!" she cried, her voice muffled. "We're both contagious!"

"You're both crazy," Sam muttered. He took down rifles resting atop a stack of boxes. "Come on. They're coming! We gotta hold them off."

Josh shook his head. "You're not making much more sense than she is," he said.

"We've all been infected," Diane said. "Your friend Sarge, the *gugwe*...they all carry this disease that Dr. Smith had created."

"Just...shut up," Sam yelled, exasperated. "Listen to me. You're not infected with nothing. Okay? Dr. Smith told me, the disease doesn't work that way.

"She should know, I guess," Diane muttered. "She *made* the disease, or helped." She looked a little calmer now, but from the look on her face, she was wrestling with Dr. Smith's credibility.

"The screamers are coming," Sam said.

"The *gugwe*, you mean?" Diane asked, almost eagerly.

"I guess...I mean, whatever you call 'em, a whole bunch of the boogers are coming down here." He thrust the rifle into Josh's hands. "You know how to shoot?"

"Are you crazy?"

Sam turned to Diane. "You?"

"I took some lessons one time," Diane said, hesitating. "I can't do it very well, but..."

"Come on out with me, then. I guess we're gonna be doing some shooting, even if we suck at it."

***

Marty heard the gunshots as his GPS guided him up Pike toward Sam Mueller's house—gunshots, and a series of deep howls that sounded like nothing he'd ever heard from an animal.

When he came in view of the house, his jaw dropped. The scene before him reminded him of some bizarre one-sided Civil War reenactment, with the part of the Confederacy played by masses of gangling, hairy monsters. Some of them were armed, and a few were stalking around purposefully, their weird doglike heads swiveling as they looked for targets. Most were in a state of agitation, leaping and shaking their arms at the sky, making those nerve-rending howls.

Two picnic tables had been set upright out in the open area before the house—Marty couldn't be sure if it could properly be called a yard. Two figures were crouched between the tables—a lone pair of humans to fill in for the Union. Both were armed, and making much better use of their rifles than the *gugwe*. Every now and then one of the monsters fell. A few of them seemed to understand that the two humans were their real enemy and kept trying to circle around the tables. Each time they were routed by a shot, but Marty thought it wouldn't be long before they broke through the puny defenses and started chowing down.

"Hey!" Suddenly, a third human was shouting as he ran, head down, toward Marty's rental. It was a young guy, his face draped in a handkerchief that had been tied clumsily behind over his mouth, like a desperado in an old movie. He was carrying a rifle, but not much more effectively than any of the monsters.

"Hey! Get back!" the kid yelled, making aggressive pushing-away gestures with both hands. "They're dangerous!"

Marty stared at him. Something about him was familiar, and from the way the kid's eyes widened when he saw him, Marty thought the feeling was mutual.

"Mr. Bloom!" the kid cried, seeming to drag the name from the recesses of his memory. He pulled the handkerchief away.

"Yeah," Marty agreed, glad he didn't have to reveal the fact he couldn't remember the kid's name. "I remember you! From the bookstore the other day! Josh, isn't it, or Jeff?"

"Josh," the kid said. "You haven't seen a woman around here? Her name's Dr. Smith. Diane is worried about her." He looked a little peeved, as though Diane should have been more worried about him.

"Right," Marty said. "And I just walked out of her office…Smith's office, I mean. One of the things nearly got me there." He didn't bother mentioning the number the *gugwe* had done on it.

At that moment, one of the *gugwe* noticed the car that had just driven up and the voices coming from it. A group of the creatures began loping toward them, moving too quickly for comfort.

"Get in!" Marty yelled, throwing open the door. The kid had no choice but to scramble inelegantly over Marty's lap. He had just enough time to get in before Marty slammed the door shut again. Then the car was surrounded by screaming, capering *gugwe*.

"So you have no idea where Smith is now?" Marty asked, eying the things nervously. One of them was hitting at the windshield with the stock of his rifle—tentatively at first, almost as if the thing were trying to figure out if it were allowed to do it. The little blows it was striking were mere love-taps compared to what it was really capable of, Marty knew. *If it takes out the windshield, we're done.*

"Sam—the guy who owns the house—he said she went that way," Josh said, pointing toward the treeline. "But he said she was acting really weird. That's what got Diane so worried."

"Imagine that," Marty muttered. He stabbed the flat of his hand down on the car's horn, wincing at the loud blare. The *gugwe* didn't much like it either; they backed away from the car, covering their ears and snarling.

"Okay, Josh, look…we've got to make it to Smith. I can't explain now, but I've got something for her. My phone on the seat there…"

"I don't see it," Josh said, searching frantically.

"I think you're sitting on it," Marty said gently. *Poor kid's got the heebie-jeebies, but good.* "Take it and call the last number under 'Recent.' That's Smith's number, I called her like forty times driving out here. I want you to keep trying her. I'm going to drive toward the trees there, get us as close to where she was as possible."

"And what then?" Josh asked, already putting through the first call.

"If we haven't found her, we'll have to go on foot. I know, I know, those things…but hopefully this'll give 'em something to think about."

With that, Marty hit the horn and the gas simultaneously. The car jumped clumsily ahead, bumping its way over the rough ground of Sam's yard. The *gugwe*—who had just begun recovering their courage—fell back again, clutching their ears and squealing. A good twenty more came running at the car, but they didn't like the horn any better than their comrades.

"Here we go," Marty said, as the car flew by masses of frightened, confused-looking *gugwe*. A weird feeling of exhilaration swept over him and he laughed. "We havin' fun yet?" he sang out.

"Dr. Smith's not answering," Josh said, pressing the CALL button. At that moment, a ringtone blared through the car—"Barracuda" by Heart.

Marty laughed. "That *can't* be her." *Why the hell do I feel so good? I should be pissing myself.*

"No, it's…that's *my* phone," Josh said, frantically juggling the two. "It's Diane. Hold on."

***

"Josh, what are you doing?" she yelled. "Whose car is that? *Where are you going*?"

Sam continued aiming and shooting while she talked. He looked more irritated than frightened, which she took an odd comfort in.

"I'm with Marty!" Josh yelled. "Your koala bear? *Stalking the Legend*? He's out here looking for Dr. Smith. The *gugwe* are…" There was a loud *bump* and Josh gasped while a voice Diane was only vaguely able to connect with the writer from the bookstore chanted, "*Whoops*, there goes another rubber-tree plant…"

"Josh, is he okay? Are you alright?"

"Better than I'd be out there with the *gugwe*. I'll call you back as soon as we find Dr. Smith, okay?"

It wasn't okay, not by a long shot, but Diane hung up and thrust the phone back into her pocket. She looked down at Daisy, who lay curled against the upright table, wagging her nail nervously.

Everything okay, Mom? Diane petted her.

"Ah, you sucker," Sam muttered, stopping to reload. "If I'd known this was coming, I'd have bought a damn machine gun."

A *gugwe*, tusks bared and eyes staring out of its horror mask face, appeared suddenly over the top of the table, reaching for Sam's head. Diane, exhibiting reflexes she hadn't known she possessed, raised her rifle and blew the top of its head off. As she stood, trembling with adrenaline, the body slumped down over the table, blood gushing out. Wincing, she prodded at its hairy shoulder with her rifle barrel, but Sam shook his head.

"Leave it there," he said. "Helps make a whadda-ya-call, a barricade. And maybe the others'll think twice before they try'n follow it." With that, his rifle now fully loaded, he went back to shooting.

Diane glanced back down at Daisy, who turned her eyes up at her and sighed. "I know, right?" she whispered. "The boys are *crazy*!"

***

The *gugwe* didn't like Dr. Smith. They made no move to hurt her or even get too close to her, but as they loped along beside her, more than a few glared viciously. The scientist in her wasn't comfortable attributing this to simple jealousy over the friendship she had enjoyed with their leader. Jealousy was a human trait, and assigning it to animals was a risky proposition.

On the other hand, she'd seen it in *gugwe* before, many times. It was the whole reason they had launched this attack on Western Pennsylvania at their leader's behest—to get to her. And even if she were to suppose Caliban's tribe had less of what he had, it would still make sense. After all, access to the alpha male was power, just as access to females was. What else should they feel, if not jealousy?

She tramped along, trying to ignore her escort, trying to ignore the constant niggling need to examine these products of her life's work with a raised eyebrow and a muttered, Spock-like "Fascinating." Instead, she kept silent.

This is where her family was from, though she hadn't grown up here. Her family had moved to Wisconsin about the time she was born, and that was where she'd been raised and educated. But Pennsyltucky still fascinated her—that was why she'd elected to make this the base of her new life after her work with Tom Wilcox's team went south. Maybe it was the mountains. They gave the whole area a weirdly primordial feel, along with the legends and folklore that suffused the local culture. She didn't even consider the fact those mountains hid a fairly robust population of hominids—Sarge's people.

And they were the ones, ultimately, she was really worried about, should the *gugwe* choose to go local. The Old People were a proud and prickly race, not at all averse to making war on a species they felt threatened their hold on the area. If the local human communities had any idea how many times that had nearly happened, real estate prices in the Keystone State would fall like a dropped *galupke*.

And if the *gugwe* and the Old People went to war…well, it wouldn't be pretty.

One of the *gugwe* had fallen in step with her, occasionally shooting glares at her. He was an old campaigner with grey in his muzzle, probably one of the generation just after Caliban's. She made a couple of quick gestures at the creature in the abbreviated sign language she used to communicate with them. *Nearly there*?

The *gugwe*, still glaring, fingered the air: *Nearly there*, it confirmed. Some of the *gugwe* understood English well enough, but of course they couldn't speak it. Neither could the Old People. That was what ultimately would destroy them, should things come to an all-out war with the local humans.

They were now facing the side of a mountain, the sides forming a rocky, gradual slope into a heavy forest of maple and oak. There was a cave just ahead, the opening yawning in the mountain face. Unlike many of the caves she remembered from her girlhood visits, this one was natural, not part of an old coal mine.

Several *gugwe* squatted outside—she could tell they were females, though most casual viewers would be hard-pressed to see the difference between them and the males. One, the leader of

Caliban's harem, came down on all fours, its eyes locked belligerently on hers.

Joyce didn't turn her eyes away. "Where is he?" she signed.

Instead of signing back, the female made a rough gesture at the cave entrance. The other members of the harem backed away, allowing her access, but a moment of caution prevented her from proceeding. The cave's ceiling was low—she'd have to enter on her hands and knees.

She trusted Caliban's people—didn't she? But if they turned on her, this would be the place to do it. And even though she still had the pistol that had taken Sam Mueller's friend away, she wouldn't give herself a high chance of survival should she be ambushed.

It was only when the harem leader gestured again, this time in sign, saying, "bad sick," that Joyce turned and, getting down and all fours, crept into the cave.

TEN

Marty had to stop at the treeline. In his hyped-up state, he came close to simply letting the accelerator and steering wheel decide how far they could make it into the forest. *Unfortunately*, he thought, putting the car in Park, *I'm not twenty-one anymore*.

"So I take it you changed your mind about *gugwe*," Josh said. He wasn't exactly smirking, but it said something that he couldn't let go of their bookstore discussion even now. *God save me from crypto-nerds*, Marty thought, almost affectionately.

"You could say that," he said out loud. "You could also say maybe we should table this discussion for a little later. For now, how about you hand me that little package in that bag there?"

"Is it a weapon?" Josh asked, glancing out the rear window as Marty took the package. "Because I think we might need one."

A contingent of *gugwe* were approaching—cautiously, but with coldly determined eyes. Marty weighed their options, which were, putting it mildly, limited. Laying on the horn might put the fear of God in them, but only for a minute or so. They couldn't stay in the car indefinitely—doing so would allow the *gugwe* to surround them.

"How good are you with that pea-shooter?" he asked, nodding at the rifle clutched in Josh's hand.

"Let's put it this way," Josh said with a laugh, handing the rifle over. "If you were a quadriplegic who'd never seen a gun before, you'd still be a better shot than me."

"Roger that," Marty said, taking the gun and looking it over. Standard-issue hunting rifle. It had been years since he'd fired one, but he should be able to fake it long enough for what he had in mind.

"Here," he said, handing Josh Wilcox's package. "Trade ya. I need you to start running. Into the woods. If the hairy-scaries out there send me to Valhalla, try your best to get that to Dr. Smith. Tell her it's from Wilcox. I don't know what else to do but that."

Josh took the package gingerly. He looked as though he were worried it might blow up in his face. He looked as though he had severe misgivings about the plan in general, but finally he nodded and slipped the package into the inner pocket in his jacket.

"Good man," Marty said, and with that they both got out of the car.

The *gugwe* in the front lines snarled and hooted, but that stopped cold when Marty fired the rifle into the air. "Ten-*hut*!" he roared.

Several of the *gugwe* growled in confusion, but a few straightened up and faced him with cold glares. Whether their intention was to defy or obey, Marty had no idea, but they didn't attack. For the moment, that was good enough for him.

"Ten-Hut!" he boomed again, projecting as well as he could an arrogant confidence.

Replies came from the mass of *gugwe*. "Hut! Hut!"

"At ease!" Marty yelled. The *gugwe* didn't noticeably relax, but Marty had the feeling they were perfectly happy to stand here receiving commands in militarese until the cows came home. Something in them recognized this. It was as comfortingly familiar to them as the words in a Mass would be to a lapsed Catholic.

Now came the hard part. Marty inhaled, then bellowed, putting everything he had into it.

"Bout…*face*!"

For a wonder, several of the *gugwe* actually swiveled around on their heels, facing the direction from which they'd come.

"Forward…*march*!"

That was when things got dicey. A large number of the *gugwe* who'd turned actually started loping back off toward Sam's house, but others seemed to realize something was off. Suspicious red eyes were turned on Marty. Several of the creatures were close enough that Marty could see their eyelids fluttering as they bared their tusks. It looked strange, and he had no idea why they were doing it…but he had a feeling it didn't bode well for him. Either his lack of confidence was somehow showing, or they simply didn't like taking orders from one of the humans they'd apparently been sent to destroy.

"Onnadouble...*march*!" By now, the group facing him had diminished by half, but the *gugwe* remaining were not happy. Several tried to obey Marty's command, but bumped into their less compliant fellows. This resulted in a lot more growls and eyelid-flutters.

Then one of the creatures in front charged without warning. It wasn't one of those packing a rifle, but the sight of it tearing toward him, bent over so far it was nearly on all fours, almost had Marty running back to the car.

Instead, he lowered the rifle, trying to take aim as calmly as possible. He'd hoped to avoid this, mainly because he had no confidence he could single-handedly take on a group of even three *gugwe*, let alone the dozen now facing him. But his options had run out.

"Bang," he whispered and pulled the trigger.

The rifle gave a hollow click, nothing more. Either Sam had forgotten to give Josh bullets, or had given him an unloaded gun, hoping it would give him some confidence without any ability to accidentally shoot his own foot off.

"Aw, crap," Marty muttered, staring into the face of the incoming *gugwe*.

***

"So how's the old man?" Joyce asked. She had always used English with Caliban, even though he could only understand a few words.

This far inside, the cave was little more than a clumsily dug tunnel, smelling of damp earth. The rough ceiling scraped against her back. There were, of course, no lights, so she had to use her cellphone. What she saw made her inhale sharply.

The old man didn't look good at all.

He was still bigger than the other *gugwe*, but he'd lost a significant amount of weight. His black fur had fallen out in patches, and what remained had gone an unhealthy-looking white. His eyes were rheumy and unseeing, and he smelled. The way he clutched at the air made Joyce suspect he wasn't really aware of her presence.

"Oh Jesus," she whispered. "Caliban..."

Suddenly, it was 1981 again and she had the world by the nuts. She was going to win a Nobel Prize as the first primatologist—hell, the first human being—to communicate in a significant way with a nonhuman. That chick who taught Koko the gorilla to sign had nothing on her. The fact that the creatures she was teaching were the products of a military-sponsored genetic-engineering program that would have given Josef Mengele a fit didn't even enter into the equation. For the first time in her life, little Joycie Kovacs had found her *work*, and his name, copped out of a tattered freshman Shakespeare anthology, was Caliban.

Caliban wasn't just an animal, though his genetic background was a wild mix of lemur, baboon, and what spare DNA the lab could scrape off Sasquatch hair. He had thoughts and could put them together into ideas. He talked to her.

How had things gone wrong so badly? So *completely*?

She reached for his arm, stroking it. "I wish I had thought to bring you some water. I'm an idiot."

Caliban's red eyes—now tinged an unhealthy yellow—stared uncomprehendingly at her. He bared his teeth, but Joyce didn't stop stroking him. *Let him bite my damn hand off. I deserve it.*

"That damned Wilcox. Hope the sonofabitch burns in hell." She didn't know what to do. Two veterinary doctorates and she had no idea how to make this creature's pain go away.

Story of my life.

Could she get him back to her office? Of course not. The idea was idiotic, but once it took root, she couldn't get rid of it. The big thing was getting him out of the cave. Once she did that, she could somehow convince the others—call them his children or followers, it didn't matter—to help her get him back to Sam's place. Sam would drive her back to her office, he'd do it unquestioningly even though she'd put a bullet in *his* monster. Because that's what people up here did—they helped when they were asked. Try finding that in New York City.

She tried to pull him by the arms, but either she was hurting him or he simply didn't know what she was doing. He made a high-pitched sound of pain and fear.

"Caliban," she said sternly, refusing to let go of his hands. She began picking words out on his fingers in sign. "Caliban, come on! You know me. It's Joyce. Joyce. Come the hell on, Caliban!"

Something lit up in his eyes for half a second.

And of course that was the moment he began slipping away for real. He did give her one thing; he reached up and clawed at the air with his misshapen fingers, muttering and hissing. Signing.

No take...wood.

He meant, *don't take any wooden nickles.* The first really complex thing he'd learn to sign, God only knew why she'd chosen such a stupid expression to teach him.

And then he was gone and Joyce went into a screaming, sobbing decompression.

***

The *gugwe* on the mountainside had already seen Josh and made no move after him, so he made no attempt to hide himself. They stared at him for a long while, scratching themselves and growling, but for whatever reason these creatures seemed lacking in aggression, unlike the ones who had attacked Sam's house, who had it in spades.

Then again, they might be waiting for orders, Josh thought. They did give that impression, though who it was who might give the orders he had no idea.

He stood on his toes, craning his head to try for as much information as possible without going any nearer. Was this where Dr. Smith was hiding herself? The cave looked awfully small, but he guessed she could have made it in.

At that moment, a loud cry echoed from the cave's mouth. At first, Josh assumed it was a *gugwe*; it seemed a natural assumption, given the volume and sheer savagery of it. But then something told him otherwise. Something about the pitch of the yell. No animal could make a noise of such mindless agony.

"Dr. Smith?" He put his hands to his mouth and yelled the name, wincing as the syllables echoed from the surrounding mountains. The only answer that came back was a series of loud, heartbroken sobs—the only confirmation he needed.

The guards on the mountainside grew agitated, leaping in place and turning themselves in idiot circles. One of them took off running down the mountain toward Josh and he tensed, tightening his grip on the stick he'd picked up in the forest.

But the *gugwe* paid him no attention, barreling past him on all fours into the forest. The other guards crept over to the cave mouth, looking for all the world like dogs gathered at their master's deathbed.

Josh had no idea what it was that sent him struggling up the mountainside. The *gugwe* by the cave mouth watched him, but their eyes seemed less hostile now. They made no attempt to run at him or attack.

When Josh got to the cave mouth, he shouted for Dr. Smith again. He *really* didn't want to go in there. A rank smell wafted out, a stink of death and decay, and he could see how narrow and cramped the cave was from where he stood.

Suddenly, Dr. Smith came out, creeping on her hands and filth-stained knees. The minute she cleared the cave's mouth, the *gugwe* guards piled into the cave.

Josh and the doctor looked at each other for a long while. Finally, Josh went and helped her to her feet. As she dusted herself off, Josh took the package Marty had given him from his jacket, offering it to her.

"I was supposed to give this to you," he said. "It's from someone named Wilcox."

Dr. Smith's mouth crooked up into a bitter smile as she took the package. "Is that right?" she said. She made no move to open it.

"*General* Wilcox?"

"I guess."

She turned the package idly in her hands, as though it were some kind of puzzle she wasn't particularly interested in solving. "He wasn't a general when I first met him, back in…oh, that was '81, '82. He was a major back then. Already on his way up, though. They'd put him in charge of the project, see. I don't think he understood exactly what they were doing. Neither did most of the scientists for that matter. Each one had their own little piece of the puzzle to work on, and they were happy to do that.

"That's how that kind of work gets done. The guy monitoring the growth of an embryo doesn't worry about what it'll look like in ten years, when it's tearing out the throat of some poor asshole on a battlefield."

Josh sank down to a sitting position, wincing at how cold and wet the ground was.

"You're talking about the *gugwe*? We looked at your journals…the ones you'd been using when you worked on Sarge."

Joyce nodded, continuing to play with the package. He had an odd idea she might simply toss it away at any moment.

"I'd been brought into the project as a consultant in primatology. I was fresh out of grad school, a rising star. Of course, you won't find my name mentioned in any of the standard texts today. Not even a footnote.

"I was as blind as any of them. Tom's big contribution was drilling the newly grown *gugwe* like recruits on Parris Island. 'Ten-hut,' and all that. Teach them to fire a rifle. I let him do it, because he wanted to do it and it was easier than having a tenth pointless confrontation with him that particular week, rather than just nine. Caliban was watching, though. He was always good at absorbing things for later use.

"He was the first. My baby, I guess. Far more intelligent than any of the others, the program's greatest success. And now…"

One by one, the *gugwe* females came out and began wailing. Their cries echoed throughout the forest, a weird, unearthly song that belonged more to the ocean than to the trees.

"I did throw a fit when he started the lab boys working on the virus, though," Dr. Smith went on. "As a 'control,' Tom said. That was when I put my foot down, little good as it did me. I mean, that part of the project was an abject failure. The only one the disease took to was Caliban, and it's taken decades to finally bring him down. But when the first symptoms showed…that was when I let them all go. Opened the cages one night, and ran. Changed my name and my occupation. Forced them to deep-six the program. Turned the mighty Tom Wilcox into a petty bureaucrat, a misinformation wrangler, hiring hack writers to tell everyone that those hairy monsters they kept seeing in the woods weren't real."

Dr. Smith shrugged. “It wasn’t much of a revenge, but you take what you can get.”

She went silent, listening to the wailing. Josh did as well. He couldn’t figure out if it was meant to be mourning or a message being broadcast far and wide, picked by and passed on individual by individual, until an entire species knew its leader was dead.

“So, can I ask,” Josh said carefully. “What was in the package?”

“A cure.” Dr. Smith smiled bitterly, lifting out something that looked like a toy raygun. “He’d been sending me messages every way he could. He’d had his intel boys on finding me, but he never pushed me too hard. I think that—and the cure—was meant as an apology.

“He finally got it to me. Too late, but that was my fault.”

***

The sound of wailing stopped the charging *gugwe* dead in its tracks. Not seeing much choice in the matter, Marty stood his ground, rifle lowered. If it started charging again, what would he do? Smack it on the nose and say, “Bad monster?”

The creature shook its head like a dog with water in its ear, grunting and looking shocked. At first, Marty thought it was staring at him, then he realized its eyes were focused on the trees behind him. Suddenly, it tore off past him, leaving him staring after it.

“Don’t say goodbye, asshole,” he muttered. Then when he turned again, the forest before him was a massive row of *gugwe*, all of them running toward him.

But it was the same story. Marty lifted his rifle, but the creatures didn't touch him, barely looked at him as they thundered past. It took some minutes for all of them to get by him, and then—apart from a few straggling *gugwe*—Marty saw a big guy and a girl with dark red hair coming toward him, a small dog running happily by their side.

"Dr. Bloom!" the girl said. "Thank God! Are you alright?"

"Right as an old man can be," Marty said. He didn't know why, but that weird feeling of almost-euphoria was back upon him.

"It was the damnedest thing," Diane said, shaking her head. "Suddenly, the *gugwe* all stopped attacking us. There was this howling noise, and then all of a sudden they were all running back here. Have you seen Josh?"

"I have a feeling he's with Smith," Marty said, turning toward the tangle of trees and disappearing *gugwe* backsides. "And the *gugwe*. Let's go find them."

The three of them—and the dog—started off through the trees, dead leaves crunching under their feet.

I don't know why I feel so good, Marty thought. *Going to a funeral, and I feel like singing.*

EPILOGUE - ONE WEEK LATER

"I have to say," Marty said, sucking ketchup off his finger. "I at least understand *why* people like the burgers."

Sam reached down to pat Sugar, who lay at his feet. She was still bandaged, but she and Daisy had made fast friends and lay curled up together. "Yeah, they're pretty good," he said gruffly. "Kinda greasy, but they give you a lot." Diane noticed that he had snuck each dog a small pinch of his burger. She smiled, pretending she hadn't seen.

Dolly's was, as usual, nowhere near packed. Two or three families and one or two solitary diners sat chewing and talking to each other in slow, deep voices, occasionally laughing.

"I wish Dr. Smith—or Dr. Kovacs—had joined us," Diane said.

"Going to have to give her time, I suspect," Marty said, reaching for his glass of Coke. "I have a feeling you'll see her back in here eventually. She's apparently a bit of a fixture in this place."

"So where will you go, Marty?" Diane asked finally.

"Oh, I might stay here a while longer," Marty said. "I think I could get to like Pennsylvania. Do a little writing, try turning out something that actually makes money without Uncle Sam's help. My place in New York is a rental, after all. Not much keeping me there. In fact, I was thinking maybe you two would like to housesit for me sometime."

"Oh my God, name the time and place," Josh cried.

"Speaking of writing," Diane said quickly, "are you sure we can't blog about this, even a *little*?" She held her thumb and index finger close together to signal exactly how little she had in mind.

"Well, you're both grownups, but I really wouldn't advise it," Marty said. "Not 'til all this has died down. Maybe Tom had a softer side than he let on, and maybe he didn't...but he's definitely got a career and a reputation to protect. It may be a little while before it's safe to talk about this. But believe me, you'll have plenty of *gugwe* reports coming out of Pennsylvania, enough to keep you blogging for a lifetime."

Silence reigned over the table for a time. Finally, Diane said, "I do hope Dr. Smith will be okay."

It was Sam who finally broke the silence. "I think she'll be alright," he said. That was all, but something in his voice made the others smile.

"Hey, any younse wanna try some gobs?" he asked, signaling the waitress. "They're okay, if you like sweet stuff'll rot your teeth out."

"My friend," Marty said, "I believe you have won over your first convert. Bring them on!"

***

They came out of the woods just as the moon had reached its highest point. Joyce had been sitting in her overgrown back yard, waiting for them. There had been no real indication that they would come, certainly no promise, not even one in sign. But somehow she had managed to make her request clear, and something told her they would honor it.

Three females, the ones who had led the mourning for Caliban, came creeping toward her. One, the harem leader, carried something bundled in an old towel. Joyce took it from them and smiled down at it. It looked quizzically up at her with strange red eyes set in an odd, muzzled face.

The infant was only a week or so old, but as large as a six-month-old human. *Gugwe* grew far faster than *Homo sapiens*, after all. The mother had died in a fight over another's male. That had been concerning to Joyce. She would have hoped by now the *gugwe* would have learned better. She'd have to make it her business to make sure they did.

"Thank you," she said respectfully, looking up from the bundle. "I'll take good care of him." Whether or not they understood her words, she couldn't tell, but they looked satisfied.

One of the females stopped in the act of creeping out of the yard, turned and signed to her. *What name*?

The question surprised Joyce a little. The *gugwe* weren't overly curious or concerned with human things like names. So far as she could tell, they didn't name their children.

But the other, apparently picking up on her friend's odd curiosity, stared at Joyce as well. *Leader*? the female said, asking the question in sign. *Leader* was what they had always called Caliban.

No, Joyce signed. *Not Leader*. She smiled and, with no way of translating the name she would give the child, spoke it aloud.

"Sarge."

END

THE BEASTS OF STONECLAD MOUNTAIN by Gerry Griffiths

Clay Morgan is overjoyed when he is offered a place to live in a remote wilderness at the base of a notorious mountain. Locals say there are Bigfoot living high up in the dense mountainous forest. Clay is skeptic at first and thinks it's nothing more than tall tales.

But soon Clay becomes a believer when giant creatures invade his new home and snatch his baby boy, Casey.

Now, Clay and his wife, Mia, must rescue their son with the help of Clay's uncle and his dog, a journey up the foreboding mountain that will take them into an unimaginable world...straight into hell!

BIGFOOT AWAKENED by Alex Laybourne

A weekend away with friends was supposed to be fun. One last chance for Jamie to blow off some steam before she leaves for college, but when the group make a wrong turn, fun is the last thing they find.

From the moment they pass through a small rural town they are being hunted by whatever abominations live in the woods.

Yet, as the beasts attack and the truth is revealed, they learn that despite everything, man still remains the most terrifying evil of them all.

CHECK OUT OTHER GREAT CRYPTID NOVELS

SWAMP MONSTER MASSACRE
by Hunter Shea

The swamp belongs to them. Humans are only prey. Deep in the overgrown swamps of Florida, where humans rarely dare to enter, lives a race of creatures long thought to be only the stuff of legend. They walk upright but are stronger, taller and more brutal than any man. And when a small boat of tourists, held captive by a fleeing criminal, accidentally kills one of the swamp dwellers' young, the creatures are filled with a terrifyingly human emotion—a merciless lust for vengeance that will paint the trees red with blood.

TERROR MOUNTAIN
by Gerry Griffiths

When Marcus Pike inherits his grandfather's farm and moves his family out to the country, he has no idea there's an unholy terror running rampant about the mountainous farming community. Sheriff Avery Anderson has seen the heinous carnage and the mutilated bodies. He's also seen the giant footprints left in the snow—Bigfoot tracks. Meanwhile, Cole Wagner, and his wife, Kate, are prospecting their gold claim farther up the valley, unaware of the impending dangers lurking in the woods as an early winter storm sets in. Soon the snowy countryside will run red with blood on TERROR MOUNTAIN.

CHECK OUT OTHER GREAT CRYPTID NOVELS

BIGFOOT WAR
by Eric S. Brown

Now a feature film from Origin Releasing. For the first time ever, all three core books of the Bigfoot War series have been collected into a single tome of Sasquatch Apocalypse horror. Remastered and reedited this book chronicles the original war between man and beast from the initial battles in Babblecreek through the apocalypse to the wastelands of a dark future world where Sasquatch reigns supreme and mankind struggles to survive. If you think you've experienced Bigfoot Horror before, think again. Bigfoot War sets the bar for the genre and will leave you praying that you never have to go into the woods again.

CRYPTID ZOO
by Gerry Griffiths

As a child, rare and unusual animals, especially cryptid creatures, always fascinated Carter Wilde.

Now that he's an eccentric billionaire and runs the largest conglomerate of high-tech companies all over the world, he can finally achieve his wildest dream of building the most incredible theme park ever conceived on the planet...CRYPTID ZOO.

Even though there have been apparent problems with the project, Wilde still decides to send some of his marketing employees and their families on a forced vacation to assess the theme park in preparation for Opening Day.

Nick Wells and his family are some of those chosen and are about to embark on what will become the most terror-filled weekend of their lives—praying they survive.

STEP RIGHT UP AND GET YOUR FREE PASS...

TO CRYPTID ZOO

Printed in Great Britain
by Amazon